SHOWCASE

# ELIZABETH LOWELL

*Love Song*

**FOR A RAVEN**

# HARLEQUIN®

TORONTO • NEW YORK • LONDON
AMSTERDAM • PARIS • SYDNEY • HAMBURG
STOCKHOLM • ATHENS • TOKYO • MILAN • MADRID
PRAGUE • WARSAW • BUDAPEST • AUCKLAND

ISBN 0-373-83709-7

LOVE SONG FOR A RAVEN

For Mary Ben,
who wanted Carlson to be happy.

# Chapter 1

The man called Raven came awake between one heartbeat and the next. He lay without moving, listening with the absolute stillness of someone whose life has depended many times on sensing shifts in wind and sea. Beneath him the *Black Star* tugged at its moorings in random motions, telling him that even within the shelter of the inlet, the water was choppy. Currents of air moaned around the boat with a wild, clean sound, the voice of a wind that hadn't touched land for thousands of miles until it reached the Queen Charlotte Islands. Now that voice spoke to mountains rising steeply from the cold ocean, mountains clad in evergreens and ferns, mountains so rugged that man had chosen to challenge the untamed sea in cedar canoes rather than to walk the cloud-wreathed, primal land.

The elemental song of wind and mountain and sea were familiar to the man who lay motionless on the oversize bunk. Raven listened for a moment longer, filed away the fact that the storm had arrived twelve hours early and fell asleep once more.

Beyond the shallow crease of the inlet, the sea was a heaving blackness churned by a reckless wind. The promise of predawn light had been reduced to a vague gloaming that barely penetrated the lowering clouds. The only relief from the seamless gray came from the pale curves of an open rowboat struggling against the wind-whipped waves.

Steering the powerful outboard engine with one hand, Janna Moran kept the bow of the boat headed on a diagonal course into the wind and waves. With the other hand she bailed out the boat, using a plastic bleach bottle whose cap had been screwed on tightly and whose bottom had been cut entirely off. Normally the half-gallon bottle with its built-in handle grip did an excellent job of keeping the boat dry. Or reasonably dry. Nothing in the islands was really *dry*. The combination of the cold northern sea and the relatively warm Kuroshio current made for nearly constant fog, mist, drizzle, rain and more rain.

Usually Janna enjoyed the liquid varieties of "Queen Charlotte sunshine," but not that morning. The wild predawn churning of water and wind had begun without warning, catching her out on the open sea. The storm that had been scheduled to arrive that evening had obviously picked up both speed and strength somewhere over the Pacific. Instead of the customary rain, brisk wind and choppy seas that had been predicted, the storm was shaping up to be a much more formidable affair.

Anxiously Janna scanned the coastline to her left. By narrowing her gray-green eyes against the wind, she could just make out the rugged wall of land rising from the dark sea. She made a soft sound of dismay as she saw that she was still well short of the opening of Totem Inlet. The last time she had looked, just before the clouds had closed down in the east, she had needed only fifteen more minutes of running time before she could turn and head into the calmer waters of the inlet. But the wind had shifted. Now both tide and wind were running heavily against her, and waves were breaking over the bow as fast as she could bail.

Even worse, the outboard motor had been acting up. At first it had been no more than hesitations in the mechanical heartbeat that were so tiny she thought she had imagined them. By the time she had passed the halfway point to the inlet's safety, the hesitations had become noticeable, more ominous. The engine had stuttered twice in as many minutes, making her own heartbeat lurch.

Janna stared toward the coastline again, wondering if she dared go in closer to the land, shortening her distance to the inlet. The memory of huge waves battering against dark cliffs on either side of Totem Inlet's opening made her reject that possibility. The course she had chosen was longer but it was also far safer.

The motor coughed, faded, caught and then died.

Suddenly the wind sounded very loud. With her heart wedging in her throat, Janna turned, braced herself on the bench seat and pulled on the starter cord with all her strength. The engine made healthy ripping noises but didn't catch. She pulled again and again and felt an almost dizzying surge of relief when the motor finally beat steadily once more. Instantly she turned the bow back into the wind and cranked the speed up a notch or two. More water would come in over the gunwale at a higher speed, but she would also get to the inlet sooner.

For a few minutes Janna made good speed. Just as her heartbeat had settled down again, the motor died without warning. She dropped the bailing bottle, grabbed the starter cord and began pulling. The motor ripped, muttered and died. Janna yanked on the cord again and again. Each time she pulled, the engine stirred but didn't fully awaken.

"Damn you, *start!*"

As though it had only been waiting for the proper encouragement, the motor ripped into life. Janna's slim fingers wrapped around the handle again, feeding gas steadily as she steered once more into the wind and the waves. Sheets of wind-driven spray broke over her, sending streamers of cold water pouring over her yellow poncho. Most of the water drained off into the boat, but some of it inevitably worked beneath the poncho's hood to slide chilly fingers down her spine and between her breasts. Inside the midcalf fisherman's galoshes she wore, her feet were soaked. So were her legs from midthigh on down.

Janna bailed rapidly—not out of any hope of staying dry, but to decrease the weight of the boat so that it didn't ride so low in the heaped waves. Water was heavier than it looked, as her left arm reminded her with each stroke of the half-gallon bleach bottle. Yet for every quart she threw back into the sea, the wind delivered more across her face.

The motor shuddered and stopped. Janna dropped the bailing bottle and pulled on the starter cord again and again. With each pull the motor made a harsh ripping noise but refused to catch. She threw a worried glance toward the coastline. It was closer. Too close. Enough light had seeped through the clouds so that she could see a distinct line of foam where breakers threw themselves at the feet of dark cliffs. There was no gap in the white line, nothing to indicate a safe place to moor short of Totem Inlet itself.

Janna squeezed the bulb leading from the gasoline reservoir to the motor. Liquid spurted invisibly. She could feel its resistance in the bulb beneath her palm. She wasn't out of gas. Whatever was causing the outboard to fail wasn't a lack of fuel. Grimly she yanked on the starting cord, putting everything she had into it.

Nothing happened.

The boat slewed sideways as a wave hit. Janna barely managed to stay aboard. Without the motor's power, the boat was at the mercy of the wind and tide. Now she was sideways to the incoming waves and being shoved toward shore at a frighteningly swift pace. She pulled hard on the cord twice more, but nothing greeted her efforts, not even the familiar coughing snarl as the motor tried and failed to keep running.

Suddenly Janna knew that it was futile to waste her energy any longer. There was no more time for her to spend pulling on the starting cord of a dead motor. She scrambled off the rowboat's stern seat and threw herself onto the middle seat. Working as quickly as her cold hands would allow, she unshipped the oars, jammed the pegs down into the oarlocks and began to row with all her strength. As she pulled on the oars, she brought the bow back around to meet the wind and waves. Immediately the boat began taking on less water.

Janna braced herself and put her back into her work, pulling in long, steady sweeps as her brothers had taught her years ago on a small lake in Washington. She watched the shoreline that lay diagonally off her stern, trying to gauge her progress by landmarks that were slowly condensing out of the cloud-wrapped dawn.

When the landmarks appeared not to move, Janna thought she was simply overanxious. She picked another landmark, counted fifty strokes and checked again. She was moving relative to the land, but just barely. The wind and the tide were simply too powerful for her to overcome; and every few seconds more water splashed into the boat, adding more weight to the already unwieldy craft. At this rate she wouldn't make Totem Inlet before her strength gave out and she was pushed onto the rocks or the rowboat was swamped in one of the larger sets of waves that humped up periodically out of the west.

For a few minutes Janna picked up the pace of the rowing, putting more space between herself and the dark cliffs that lined the edge of the sea. Always before now she had thought of herself as being reasonably strong and physically competent, the legacy both of a healthy body and the goading of three muscular brothers who had teased her mercilessly when she was too weak or too slow or too timid to play their rough-and-tumble games. She had learned to smile and joke as though she didn't hurt; and she had learned to work harder and longer so that the next time she played she would be better. As a result, she had gained a reputation as a good sport with a great sense of humor.

Water sloshed ankle-deep through the boat. Janna permitted herself to look at the shoreline. She had made almost no progress. If anything, she was afraid she had drifted closer to the cliffs. For an instant fear burst in her, taking the strength from her arms. Then she set her teeth, headed the rowboat straight out to sea instead of on a diagonal course and rowed hard. After a hundred strokes the shoreline had receded somewhat. The inlet, however, was no closer.

Janna changed course slightly, choosing a heading that would bring her closer to the inlet. As she rowed she thought over her choices. Rowing straight out to sea would keep her off the rocks but wouldn't get her to safety. Rowing a diagonal course would bring her closer to the inlet, but combined with the pressure of tide and wind, it would bring her closer to the shore, as well. It would be a race to see whether the tide and wind shoved her onto the rocks before she reached the relative shelter of the inlet. Frankly, she didn't think she would make it.

And if she didn't stop rowing to bail, she would sink before she reached either cliffs or inlet.

Janna dropped the oars, bailed frantically for a minute, then whipped off her waterproof poncho and dumped it at her feet. It the boat were capsized or swamped, she didn't want to be weighed down by the unwieldly slicker. As she reached for the oars her long, cinnamon hair fanned out wildly in the wind for an instant, only to be plastered darkly against her skull when an unusually big wave burst over the gunwale. She picked up the oars and brought the bow into the waves once more. As she rowed she kicked out of the fisherman's boots, knowing they would drag her down if she tried to swim in them. She left her soaking sneakers in place; she would need them if she got to the rocky shore.

"Not *if*," Janna said firmly to herself. "*When*. You're a strong swimmer. Just two weeks ago you swam for about a mile without a break. It's not even a quarter of a mile to the inlet's mouth."

What she didn't say aloud was that two weeks ago when she had been swimming, it had been a rare, calm, hot day, and she had been in a very sheltered inlet, where the sea was as flat as a mirror. Right now the sea was neither sheltered nor calm. But there was no point in dwelling on reasons to be afraid. She knew that in dangerous situations, panic killed more people than anything else.

Pushing every other thought out of her mind, Janna bent to the oars once more. As she rowed, the fluorescent orange of her life vest swayed like a flame in the postdawn gloom. She was the only spot of life and color showing on either land or sea.

Raven stood on the stern of the *Black Star*, looking as broad shouldered and powerful as the mountains that rose steeply on either side of Totem Inlet. Beneath his feet the stern shifted and bounced slightly on the inlet's choppy waters. He stood easily, swaying as necessary to compensate for the boat's restless surges, oblivious to the chilly wind that tugged at the open collar of his midnight-blue flannel shirt. Eyes closed, he strained to hear the faint ripping sound that would tell him that the distant motor had finally caught and held. Nothing came to him but the shivering moan of the wind as it curled between the inlet's rocky walls.

He stared up the inlet through powerful binoculars, his black eyes searching the water for any sign that the boat had reached safety. There was nothing ahead but the same tiny whitecaps and choppy little waves that slapped against the *Black Star*. Beyond the inlet's mouth he could see a line of churned water. The powerful binoculars brought every detail close. Whoever was out in the descending storm would have his hands full, especially if he were in a rowboat with a dead outboard motor.

On the other hand, Raven knew that the sound of the engine could have been carried away by the capricious wind. He could be standing there imagining more problems than existed in the storm-tossed dawn. Few people other than professional fishermen came to the western side of the Charlottes. The tourists who came to the forbidding cliffs and narrow inlets either came with guides or had enough skill to sail to the islands on their own boats. They didn't come in rowboats, either—and the sounds he had heard earlier had come from a single outboard engine.

That was why Raven wondered if he were imagining things. Few people had either the skill or the foolishness to take on the west side of the Charlottes in an open rowboat. Yet it was possible that one of the Haidas from Old Masset or Skidegate had chosen to make a personal pilgrimage to Totem Inlet. The descendant of people who had routinely raided as far south as Oregon in their dugout cedar canoes wouldn't hesitate to put out to sea in a rowboat in order to reach Totem Inlet at the first stirrings of dawn.

A corner of Raven's mouth curled into a faint smile. Of course it was possible that a Haida had come to the legendary inlet for personal reasons. That was what he was doing. He had come here in his season of discontent as though he could fish satisfaction from the dark veils of the past just as he had fished silver salmon from the green veils of the sea.

Yet satisfaction had eluded him.

With the ease of years of practice, Raven put his own personal needs aside and concentrated on listening to the wind's flexible voice. From the faint, fitful sounds that had awakened him, he knew that the boat was beyond Totem Inlet's mouth. Unless the motor had started again, the man would be forced to row against the wind and tide in order to reach safety.

Unconsciously Raven flexed his big work-hardened

hands around the binoculars. If he were the man in the boat, he would be rowing right now, pulling hard on the long oars, feeling the power of his body sweeping down through the wood into the heaving sea. The boat would be cutting through the waves with deceptive ease, sliding closer to the inlet with each movement of the oars through the water.

But Raven was not the man rowing. If he had been, he would have been close enough by now to be spotted by someone standing in the inlet. There was nothing for Raven to see, however. Obviously the person out beyond the inlet lacked Raven's strength or his under-standing of the danger of letting a small boat drift too close to the unforgiving shore while he worked over a motor that was well and truly dead.

Several times Raven thought he heard faint shivers of sound that could have come from a motor. Each time he caught his breath, willing the sound to hold, to strengthen. Each time the sound vanished before he could be sure it had been his ears rather than his imag-ination that had heard it.

The wind flexed, paused and then blew with a new, sustained roar from a slightly different angle. Raven moved even as the wind did, listening intently, staring out across the chop with dark eyes accustomed to all the moods of the sea. Nothing moved within the binocu-lars's broad sweep but waves and wind. Whoever was out there simply wasn't getting any closer to safety.

If anyone were out there at all.

Yet even as the thought came, Raven discarded it. With a certainty that transcended words, he knew that someone was out on the open sea, caught between the storm and the unyielding shore. He leaped to the deck of the powerboat with a speed and lightness that was unexpected in a man of his size. From the stern locker he pulled out a long rope. He tied one end to the stern cleat. In a continuation of the same motion he threw off the stern mooring line. A few seconds later the bow line was off. At his touch the two powerful inboard engines snarled into life.

Minutes later Raven was approaching the mouth of the inlet. Windblown spray sheeted across the bow as the *Black Star* surged out into the unprotected water. Raven handled the bucking, shuddering boat with the assurance of a man born and raised on the surface of the world's biggest ocean. Braced against the hammering waves, steering with one hand and his powerful thighs, he brought the binoculars to his eyes and swept the area where he thought the boat should be.

There was nothing but water being ripped apart by the wind.

Raven widened the search, feeling minutes slipping away, knowing intuitively that his worst fears were true: someone was out there, someone whose danger increased with every second. Raven couldn't spot him, despite the fact that the waves were barely big enough to hide a rowboat in their trough. Yet the water was more than rough enough to be coming in over the gunwales with every wave, rough enough to swamp a small boat before Raven could find it.

"Come on, come on, show me where you are," Raven muttered. "It's bad out here, but not that bad. You shouldn't have swamped this quick even if you don't have much time to spare for bailing."

After several more sweeps with the glasses showed nothing, Raven brought the *Black Star* onto a different heading, one that would take him farther from the inlet and closer to shore. The boat wallowed protestingly as it presented its stern to the wind and waves. A few minutes of that twisting, cork-screwing motion would have sent most people to the nearest rail with a bout of seasickness, but Raven noticed the motion only in that it made controlling the boat while looking through the binoculars almost impossible.

Just when he was ready to switch to a different heading, he caught a flash of color off toward shore. He frowned even as he turned slightly. The flash had been too close to shore and too far away from the inlet's mouth to be the boat he was looking for. More likely it was a fishing float or crab-pot marker that had torn loose in the storm.

The flash of color came again. Raven focused and saw someone straining over oars. The rowboat vanished from sight in the trough of a wave, then reappeared in a burst of spray. Instantly Raven realized that the man was in real trouble. He obviously wasn't strong enough to make headway against the tide, wind and waves, which had pushed him dangerously close to shore. In fact, he looked more like a teenager than a man. His shoulders weren't broad, nor were his arms muscular.

Abruptly Raven began to swear, his words as savage as the wind. He threw the binoculars aside and slammed the throttle forward, sending the *Black Star* leaping toward the smaller boat. That wasn't a man out there nor even a boy; it was a woman, and she was pulling her heart out against the relentless sea. Her rowboat wallowed and rolled sluggishly, bringing the gunwale perilously close to the water. Both the woman's fear and her determination were in every straining line of her body as she fought to keep the waterlogged boat on a safe course, away from the dangerous shore.

Raven sent the *Black Star* on a broad curve that

brought him close to the rowboat. He saw the look of stunned relief on the woman's face when she spotted him. Easing closer, he cut the throttle and abandoned the wheel long enough to throw coils of the heavy towline over to the rowboat. He held his breath while the woman scrambled to the bow and made the line fast.

Only then did he notice how much water filled the rowboat. It was all but awash. He started to yell at the woman to bail, only to see the pale flash of a bleach bottle as she bent to work. Very carefully he eased the throttles up on the *Black Star,* taking slack from the towline. He felt the slight jerk as the rowboat's weight hit the end of the long line. Slowly, carefully, he began towing the rowboat toward the inlet.

Once both boats had settled into the new motion, Raven picked up the binoculars and turned toward the crippled rowboat thirty feet astern. For minutes that seemed like years, he divided his attention between steering the *Black Star* and watching the woman bail. Despite her efforts, the rowboat still rode far too low in the water for safety.

Suddenly the woman stopped bailing. Raven's mouth flattened as he watched her slump on the bench seat. Didn't she know that the danger wasn't over? The rowboat was wallowing like a pig in mud. When the time came to make the turn into the inlet, the rowboat's stern would be presented to the waves. There was no help for it, for there was no other way to get into the inlet. Unless she got to work the first wave that broke over the stern would send the rowboat right to the bottom.

And unless Raven cut the towrope as soon as the rowboat went under, he stood a good chance of going down with her.

Even as the thought came, Raven kicked out of his waterproof boots. Unconsciously his hand went to his belt for an instant. The worn, leather-wrapped hilt of his sheath knife nestled against his palm in cool reassurance.

"Bail!" Raven yelled, his voice as deep as the thunder of waves breaking over rocks.

A gust of wind ripped the word from his mouth and flung it back at him. Cursing, he stared through the binoculars. The woman seemed to be wrestling with something, but he was damned if he could figure out what it might be. Finally her struggles caused her to turn slightly, bringing her hands into the viewing field of the binoculars. She was prying at the fingers of her left hand, which were wrapped around the handle of the bleach bottle in a death grip.

Raven saw the muscles of the woman's left arm locked in a rigid spasm of protest over the demands that had been made on them. The arm was useless and would remain that way until the muscles uncramped. He saw tears of frustration welling from the woman's eyes as she fought her own body. Then he saw the brutal lines of exhaustion that had drawn her mouth into a harsh line and the blue-tinged pallor of her skin that warned of a body dangerously chilled. She was past the end of her physical strength, stripped to the core, all reserves spent.

Yet still she fought, refusing to quit.

A chill went over Raven, tightening his scalp in primal response. He had never seen anything quite so beautiful as the woman's courage. She was outmatched, overpowered, overwhelmed, yet she drove her slender body to work still harder, refusing to give up. Raven called to her as though he could give her some of his immense strength through an outpouring of words. He doubted that she understood him across the thirty feet of wind-churned sea, but he called to her anyway, wanting her to know that she wasn't alone.

When the woman finally managed to shift the bleach bottle to her right hand, Raven let out a hoarse shout of triumph. She began bailing with jerky, mechanical strokes, sending water sloshing out into the sea. He turned, adjusted the course of the *Black Star* and looked back again. Small plumes of water shooting over the rowboat's gunwale reassured him that the woman was still bailing.

With agonizing slowness the *Black Star* pulled the waterlogged rowboat toward the safety of the inlet. Raven checked through the binoculars every few moments. The water level inside the boat had gone down some, but not nearly enough for safety. He cut back his speed as much as he could and still hold his own against the storm. Although he wanted to reach the inlet's shelter as soon as possible, he had to wait while the woman bailed. If he tried to turn into the inlet now, the rowboat would capsize and sink.

Helplessly Raven watched through the binoculars as the woman struggled against the storm. The sight of her made agony twist deep inside him. It was too much like a time eight years ago, when he had watched helplessly as the woman he loved slid further and further into alternating bouts of rage and despair. He had tried to reach Angel with words of comfort and hope, tried to tell her that he loved her. He had wanted her to shift the focus of her love from a dead man to himself, from death to life. Later, when he understood that Angel was slowly killing herself rather than face life without the man she loved, Raven had realized that he wanted Angel to live more than he wanted her to love him. He had gone to her, dragged her brutally from her shell of despair—and had gotten his wish. Angel had gathered her courage and her strength. She had lived. In time she had even loved again.

But the man she loved was not Carlson Raven.

The sad memories flickered like distant lightning at the edge of Raven's consciousness, memories called up by the violence of his feelings of fury and helplessness as he watched the unknown woman struggle against the storm and her own overwhelming exhaustion. He had spent a lifetime in a body so powerful that people automatically stepped back when they first saw him; yet that power couldn't do a damn thing to help the woman now, any more than it had helped Angel long ago. It seemed to be the story of his life. Intimidating strength, a hard face, and beneath it a yearning that was as unexpected as it was enduring.

Raven's mouth flattened making the blunt lines of his face even more pronounced. The speed of the woman's bailing had fallen to nothing. Raven knew that soon she wouldn't even be keeping up with the water coming in over the gunwale. Ready or not, safe or not, he had to make the turn for the inlet.

He eased the *Black Star* in a long, shallow curve that eventually, gently swung the rowboat in a direct line into the inlet. As soon as both boats were headed straight into the narrow opening, he turned and watched the rowboat through the binoculars. Now was the time of greatest danger, when the rowboat's broad, low stern was presented to the waves. The woman knew it, too. He could tell by her uneven, almost convulsive motions as she drove her exhausted body to bail just a few more times, just a few more minutes, just a few more yards, just…

Cold blue-green water humped up and welled over the stern as the rowboat wallowed into Totem Inlet's mouth. The gunwale was so low that the wave barely foamed as it rolled over the rowboat. The boat wavered, rocked wildly and turned over with shocking speed, trapping the woman beneath as it sank.

Raven threw the binoculars aside, slammed the throttles into neutral and slashed the towrope. An instant later he hit the water in a long dive that took him halfway to the white swirl of sea that had once been a rowboat.

Nothing floated on the surface in front of him but a single oar.

## Chapter 2

Janna had no warning. One instant she had her head down as she bent over to bail out the water that was slopping around her ankles. The next instant the world tilted wildly. She tried to throw herself clear as the boat capsized, but her cramped legs responded much too slowly. It was the same for her arms. Instinctively she flung them out as though to break a fall, but only managed to jam the steering arm of the outboard engine through the armhole of her life vest.

The bottom of the boat flipped over her, shutting out the light. Even as chilled as she was the water felt cold. She was dragged over as the motor turned with the boat. In the water and darkness she was disoriented, tangled with the engine, not knowing in which direction lay freedom. With a feeling of horror she realized that the boat was sinking deeper into the cold sea, pulling her down with it despite her struggles.

Suddenly Janna was caught from behind. Something clamped around her arm and yanked. The life vest ripped away, freeing her. She was spun around, pushed down and then jerked upward.

Where there had been only darkness beneath the boat, now Janna saw far above her a silver disk that shimmered and beckoned. Feebly she tried to swim upward, for instinct and intelligence both told her that if she broke through that silver light there would be air and warmth on the other side. Even as she struggled, she realized dimly that she was going up far faster than her own efforts could account for.

Janna burst through the radiant disk and began to drag air into her aching lungs, breathing in great rasps of sound. Gradually she realized that she wasn't alone. She was being supported by a man's big hands. Eyes as dark and deep as a midnight sea were watching her. Above those unflinching eyes a thick growth of raven-black hair was slicked against a skull whose bones were as powerful and uncompromising as the hands that were holding her above the inlet's choppy waves.

As though her eyes focusing on him were the signal he had been waiting for, the man turned Janna gently in his hands and brought her shoulder blades across his chest. He held her in place by putting his right arm between her breasts until she was pinned to his chest. His arm was thick, almost overwhelming in its implicit strength. She sensed a stirring behind her, felt her body floating, and then a deep swirl of water boiled up as powerful legs scissor-kicked, propelling her and the man through the water.

With a feeling of vast relief, Janna stopped fighting the cold and the sea, giving herself wordlessly to the stranger's strength.

"That's it," said a very deep voice in her ear. "Relax. You're safe."

Like everything else Janna had seen of the stranger, the voice was strong, big, dark.

"We're almost to my boat."

The words growled against her ear like stones tumbled by storm waves. She tried to answer but found the effort beyond her. Words swirled around in her mind without connecting. Dimly she realized that she was no longer cold. At some point she had just gone numb all the way to her core, losing all feeling.

"I've got to climb on board. Hold on to the ladder until I pull you up. Can you do that?"

The world turned lazily around Janna. Black eyes came slowly into focus.

"Did you hear me?"

Janna stared at the man, wondering what he wanted from her. When she saw her left hand being tugged through the rungs of a sea ladder, she felt a bizarre impulse to laugh. A big, tanned hand wrapped her fingers around a rung. He reached for her right hand, only to encounter the drowned bleach bottle.

"You can let go now," he told her. "You don't need it anymore. You're safe."

The voice rumbled and reverberated down Jenna's spine like distant thunder, reaching her on a level deeper than intelligence, sinking down to touch the same instinct that had made her keep on fighting even when she had no more strength. She accepted the absolute truth of the stranger's words. She was safe. She had known she was safe from the instant she had felt his strong hands pushing her up into the life-giving air.

Slowly, painfully, Janna's fingers unlocked, letting the bleach bottle go. It sank swiftly, a pale shadow fading into the depths of the sea. Under the man's urging she wrapped her fingers around the ladder and hung on. She saw him grasp the low metal railing that ran along the gunwale of the boat. Muscles rippled and bunched while he pulled himself out of the water as casually as she would have stepped from the street to the sidewalk. Before she had a chance to absorb the implications of that kind of strength, she felt herself lifted from the sea and carried into a small cabin as though she weighed no more than a puff of wind.

"Hang on to me."

Janna obeyed as the world shifted again. Vaguely she realized that her feet were resting on something solid. In the next moment her knees gave way. Only the strong arm around her waist kept her from pitching face-first onto the deck. She clung to the man with numbed hands as he shifted the engines from neutral and slapped the throttles up. A throaty roar came in response. The boat surged forward, racing up the inlet.

For long minutes there was only the thunder of powerful engines and the unwavering strength of the man supporting her. Then the engines were shut off. He let go of her just long enough to moor the boat and then he returned. He began stripping off her clothes with swift, casual motions. She blinked and pushed vaguely at his hands. It was like trying to hold back the tide with a sigh. Desperately she reached for more strength, but every bit she had was already involved in the huge shudders that were racking her body.

"Don't fight me, small warrior," he rumbled gently. "You'll never get warm in those soaking clothes."

Janna looked at the man with confused, gray-green eyes, wanting to ask who he was and how she had gotten there and why she was so terribly cold. Nothing came out but an odd whimper as the last of her strength bled away and the world darkened around her.

Raven caught her against his body, peeled off the remainder of her clothes and carried her to his oversize bunk. The sight of her pulse beating against the smooth curve of her neck reassured him, but her skin was far too cold. He yanked back the blankets from her bunk and dried her as best he could before he slid her between the sheets. He pulled off his clothes with harsh sweeps of his hands, ripping cloth in his haste. Pausing only long enough to jerk a special blanket from a cupboard, he crawled into the bunk with her.

"I don't know if you can hear me," Raven said as he arranged the woman on top of his big body, "but you're going to be warm again. This survival blanket takes every bit of our heat and reflects it back to us. It wouldn't do you much good by yourself, but as long as I'm wrapped up with you it's better than a bonfire. I'm too damn big to be chilled by a few minutes in a summer ocean."

There was no response from the woman but the convulsive shuddering of a body that had been pushed too hard and now was too cold to warm itself. Raven shook out the survival blanket and wrapped both of them within its thin, flexible folds. The inner, heat-reflecting side of the blanket gleamed in shades of silver. The outer, heat-absorbing side of the blanket was a midnight blue as dark as the sodden flannel shirt that lay in shreds on the deck by the bunk.

Long shudders of the woman's body threatened to shake off the blanket. Raven's hands moved gently over her, both soothing and slowly rubbing warmth back into her clenched muscles. After a long time her body began to relax as the violence of her shivering waned. He shifted slightly, bringing her into more complete contact with the heat of his body. She murmured and instinctively burrowed closer to the abundant warmth that was radiating into her.

Raven's hands gently massaged the long, slender back to the swell of the woman's buttocks. The firm, deep muscles were still cool to his touch but no longer chilled. She was bruised, numb, exhausted, but no longer in danger of succumbing to hypothermia. He smiled and felt a sense of satisfaction that for once his body had been good for something more than drawing sideways stares from strangers. He wondered if the woman would be frightened when she awoke and saw what had fished her from the sea.

He hoped not. Even half-drowned and utterly exhausted, she had looked sleek and very feminine beneath the soggy clothes. She also felt amazingly good in his arms, fitting against his body with a perfection that would have shortened his breath in other circumstances and was threatening to do so even now. Her hips swelled smoothly beneath his hands. Her breasts were soft and her nipples were as hard as pebbles against his chest. He wondered if she would respond like that to heat rather than cold—a man's heat. Would she come to a man with the same elemental passion and courage with which she had faced the storm?

The thought chased the last of the cold from Raven's body. He felt a surge of hot, sweet heaviness in his blood. Abruptly he cast his willpower over his glittering, leaping thoughts as though they were wild salmon coming to the net. She had trusted him enough to give herself over to his keeping despite the fact that he must have looked almost as frightening as the sea to her. He would no more violate that trust than he would have let her drown before his eyes.

"Can you hear me yet?" he asked softly, feeling his own deep voice rumble in his chest. "You're going to be fine. A few hours of sleep, some warm food, a few lazy days, and you'll be ready to tackle me with one hand tied behind your back."

The thought of anyone taking him on like that made Raven smile. He was still smiling when the woman's head stirred and wide eyes studied him through dense eyelashes. At close range her eyes were the color of a cedar forest veiled by silver fog. They were deep, intelligent, exquisitely clear.

Janna blinked, trying to connect the resilient warmth beneath her with the clear, oddly gentle black eyes that were so close to her own.

"You're very warm," she said slowly, grappling with each word through a haze of exhaustion.

"You aren't," he said, amusement clear in his deep voice as he ran his palm down to her cool, naked thigh.

"I know." She sighed and let her head sag onto his chest, too exhausted to keep her eyes open any longer. "What…happened?"

"Sleep," he said softly as he pulled the survival blanket up over her wet hair. "You'll remember when you wake up."

Raven felt her breath wash over him with reassuring warmth. Her body changed subtly, taking on the heaviness of utter relaxation. Before she took another breath she was asleep. The trust implied by that simple act washed over Raven in another kind of warmth until it was a subtle radiance shimmering within the darkest reaches of his mind. His breath sighed out to mingle with hers. He fell asleep with the scent of the woman and the sea reaching out to him, surrounding him.

* * *

Janna woke slowly. With one hand, she reached out, fumbling for the control on her electric blanket. She must have been very cold when she went to bed last night; she had left the dial on high. Even her pillow was hot. Blindly her fingers began searching for the control that hung over the mattress midway down the bed. What she found was smooth, firm, resilient, as hot as satin left out in the sun. She searched the surface with sleepy curiosity, wondering if she were still dreaming. Something stirred beneath her touch.

"Careful, woman. You're fishing in rocky waters."

Janna's eyes flew open and her head came up in a rush as she propped herself on her elbow. An odd, silvery blanket slithered aside with her sudden motion, revealing an expanse of bare male chest that was frankly intimidating—or would have been if she hadn't grown up with men nearly as large. Black hair gleamed in a neat wedge that tapered swiftly to a dark line bisecting a very large, very powerful body. Farther down the hair fanned out into a black tangle. That was where her hand was. Her fingers weren't resting in that tangle of masculine hair. Not quite.

With a gasp, Janna yanked back her hand. "I'm sorry, I…I…" Suddenly she realized that she was as naked as the giant who had stirred beneath her touch. She had been lying half on, half off his body, her breasts nestled against the muscular swell of his arm. "Who… what?"

"People here call me Raven," he said in a voice so deep that it vibrated down her spine. "As for what—"

"Never mind," she interrupted quickly, feeling a blush crawl from her breasts to her cheeks. "I might have gone crazy, but I haven't forgotten eighth-grade science."

"Science?" he asked, as he reached for the survival blanket that was sliding farther away with every instant.

"Human reproduction," she said succinctly.

Raven's laughter sent odd shivers through Janna. It was such a rich sound, as warm and textured as his very masculine flesh had been beneath her fingertips.

Janna's blush deepened at the sensual direction of her own thoughts. The cold water must have frozen what passed for her brain.

Abruptly memories exploded. Cold. Storm. Water. A silver disk floating impossibly far above her head. Everything came rushing back on Janna with dizzying force. She stared at the man lying so close to her. Strong hands. Black eyes. A voice like waves breaking over rocks, yet somehow warm, caressing. She had known it instinctively. She was safe with him.

"You saved my life."

"You fought with everything you had in you and them some," Raven said. "I just gave you a little hand."

Janna looked at the broad, dark, strong hand holding the strange blanket, pulling it up over her, tucking her within its warm folds. She would have died out in the storm if it hadn't been for those strong hands. She knew it.

"Little?" she repeated softly. "There was nothing little about it."

Raven held up his hand as though he had never seen it before and nodded. "You're right. There's nothing little about it," he said, deliberately misunderstanding. As casually as though he were alone, he leaned forward until he could flip the dark blue bed sheet up over his naked hips. "Warm enough?" he asked, looking at her with concern.

"Yes. Thank you." Even as Janna spoke, more memories

came. She had been so cold she could barely feel the deck beneath her feet. She had been unable to stand, to swim, even to breathe. "I...if it hadn't been for you..."

With a shrug of massive shoulders, Raven said, "I've always been bigger than the people around me. It's good to know that I'm useful for more than pulling nets and scaring children."

Janna blinked, sensing the loneliness beneath the matter-of-fact words. For all his rough looks and over-whelming male power, Raven was not an insensitive man. Impulsively she put her hand on the bunched strength of his shoulder. "I'll bet the children run toward you, not away," she said softly. "They know they'll be safe with you. I knew it," she added, gray-green eyes searching his. "Raven, I don't know how to thank—"

"You must be thirsty," he said, cutting off her words.

Janna suddenly realized two things: Raven didn't want her thanks, and she was thirsty. Her throat felt as though it were lined with sandpaper. "Yes," she said, hearing the rasp in her own voice.

"Swallowing saltwater will do it to you every time. I've got tea, coffee, water or soup."

"Tea. Please."

Janna tried not to watch as Raven rolled out of the bunk in a single coordinated movement, taking the sheet with him. She tried, but not looking at him was impos-sible. He was so big that he filled the cabin. On him, the navy blue cloth he wrapped casually around his hips looked the size of a beach towel rather than a bed sheet. She had come from a family of big men, and at five feet nine inches wasn't exactly small herself; but the man called Raven was a giant.

He was also compelling in the same wild, primitive

way that the surrounding land was compelling. The naked strength and endurance in him tugged at her senses, as did the laughter and solitude that gleamed deep within his black eyes. Potent, vital, alone, Raven called to her at levels she hadn't even known she had until she had awakened with his life's heat radiating through her.

What a pity she didn't call to him in the same way.

Janna's mouth curved down in a sad smile. She had awakened naked in bed with the most intriguing man she had ever met, and he had treated her like a sister even after her hand had blundered into such intimate contact with his body. She was used to being treated like a sister. After all, she was one. Sister to three strapping brothers. That didn't bother her. Being treated like a sister by her ex-husband—that *had* bothered her.

Wryly Janna conceded that she shouldn't be surprised that Raven hadn't been physically intrigued by her. She blew a limp, damp string of hair away from her nose and sighed. She had no illusions as to how she looked under the best of circumstances. Striking was what her family said. Privately, Janna had decided that was what people told tall women they liked who didn't possess the soft, blond, kittenish looks that men invariably preferred. Having just been fished from the sea half-drowned and blue with cold, Janna knew she must look about as appealing as a beached jellyfish.

No wonder Raven hadn't wanted her gratitude. The poor man must have been terrified that she would offer to pay him off in bed. Again Janna smiled wryly. He had reason to worry. He wouldn't have gotten any great bargain from accepting her offer. Experienced she was not. She could count on one hand the number of times her husband had made love to her during their short "marriage."

"Such sad eyes," Raven said. "Worrying about what happened? Don't. You're safe now. I'll take you back to civilization as soon as the storm blows over. As for your boat…" he shrugged. "I'll see that you get a new one. And a decent engine to go with it."

Janna's eyelashes swept down, concealing her emotions. Then the comment about the engine penetrated. Her eyes opened wide as she looked up at Raven. "How did you know that the engine gave me trouble?"

"Nobody rows the west side of the islands in a storm for the sheer joy of it," Raven said dryly. "One lump or two?"

"I feel like I've already taken fifty," Janna said, rubbing her left arm. "Two lumps, please. How did you know I liked sugar in my tea?"

"You look like a woman who enjoys her senses," he said matter-of-factly. "Is your arm still cramped?"

"Was it cramped?" asked Janna, looking at her left arm with new interest and wondering what Raven had meant about her enjoying her senses.

"Don't you remember?"

Janna frowned, drawing dark cinnamon eyebrows down in soft, twin curves. "I remember that damned engine quitting and starting and quitting until finally it went dead. I remember rowing." She looked at her hands. They were red, chafed and blistered here and there from the rough oar handles. "I remember being cold."

"Do you remember bailing?"

"Sure. Every chance I got." She grimaced. "It wasn't often enough, though."

"What do you remember after you saw the *Black Star*?"

Janna looked around at the beautifully finished interior

of the boat. "Is this the *Black Star*?" she asked, indicating the boat with her hand, then yanking the blanket hurriedly into place as it slithered down her breasts.

Raven nodded. With an effort of will he kept from staring at the corner of the blanket, where one nipple peeked invitingly from beneath the silver folds. The blush that had risen up Janna's clear, flawless skin when she had realized that she was naked and in bed with a stranger had told Raven that she wasn't accustomed to waking up that way. Her curious, incendiary touch as she explored his rapidly hardening flesh had told him that she wasn't accustomed to men, period. Nor was she a child. He guessed that she was in her early twenties. Most women her age would have known instantly what that particular part of a man's anatomy felt like between the sheets. She hadn't.

That had been all that had kept Raven from returning the favor, running his hand down her warm, supple body to discover the heat deep inside her. He was sure that sensual heat was there, and he was sure that she would give it to him if he asked. She was so damned grateful for being fished out of the inlet.

Raven's mouth turned down in a hard curve. He wasn't that kind of predator, despite his name and his looks. He wouldn't take advantage of her gratitude. The woman with the sad eyes and brave smile wasn't a predator, either. Once the emotions of the instant wore off, she would regret having given in gratitude what she had been born to give in love.

But not to him. Experience had taught Raven that he just wasn't the kind of man that women loved. He was too big. Too hard. Too rough. Too Indian. To make it worse, he was invariably attracted to his opposite—like the deliciously soft, wonderfully supple woman he had found fighting the sea. Usually such women proved to be disappointing in other ways, lacking the core of humor and courage that he valued far more than he valued mere looks.

Angel had been different. She had discovered in herself enough raw courage for ten people. And so had the woman he had pulled from the sea, the woman watching him now with clear, silver-green eyes. Trusting him.

Gently Raven tucked the blanket in around Janna's shoulders, concealing the tempting pink nipple from sight. "Do you feel like breakfast?" he asked.

"Gee, I don't know. Do I look like breakfast?" she shot back, embarrassed to realize that she had been hanging out of the blanket like a ripe raspberry and all he could think of was covering her up. Then she heard her own words all but demanding that Raven notice her nakedness. She groaned at the flush climbing up her cheeks once more. "You saved the body, but I'm afraid you left the brains at the bottom of the inlet."

"I'll look for them when I fish for dinner," Raven promised blandly, but his eyes gleamed like polished jet. "Do you have a name, or are you like the shamans, giving your true name to no one?"

"Janna Moran," she said. She eased her right arm cautiously out from beneath the slippery blanket and held out her hand. "And you're—Raven?"

"Yes," he said, taking her hand.

For a moment they smiled at each other, silently recognizing the incongruity of introducing themselves after they had awakened naked in one another's arms. Janna's fingers looked slender and very feminine against the weathered toughness of Raven's hand. He remembered how those fingers had felt exploring him sleepily.

"Is that a first or a last name?" Janna asked as Raven released her hand and turned away quickly.

"When I fill out forms for the government, it's a last name, and Carlson is my first name. Otherwise, Raven is the name most people use."

He hesitated, thinking of Angel. She and Grant had called him Carlson. But Grant was dead. Only Angel called him Carlson now—and Miles Hawkins, Hawk, the man Angel loved. Hawk called him Carlson, too.

Raven smiled slightly, remembering how he had felt when he had discovered the depth of Angel's love for another man. He supposed he should have hated Hawk, but hatred was impossible. Hawk had given Angel the very heart of life. Raven loved him for that as he had never loved another man.

"But not everyone calls you Raven," Janna said softly, seeing the bittersweet smile on Raven's lips. Janna wanted to ask who the woman was who could make Raven smile with such love and sadness, but Janna said nothing. It was enough to know that there was a woman, and love and sadness. "What shall I call you?"

"Raven. It's how I think of myself, now."

Janna smiled, feeling somehow as though she had received a gift.

"Raven," Janna said, liking the feel of the name on her tongue.

Raven smiled down at Janna, wondering what thoughts moved in the shadowed depths beneath the clear silver-green of her eyes. The smile she gave him in return was open, friendly, engaging, humorous. It was also subtly different from the ones he had seen before he tucked the blanket around her shoulders. Part of Janna's personality was now concealed, the part that had shimmered just beneath the surface of her eyes when she looked at him and saw the man who had pulled her from the cold water.

Raven frowned slightly, feeling as he always did when he saw life flashing just below the green surface of the sea, life turning and diving for the cool, safe depths, life sliding away from his presence. Somehow, something beautiful and fragile had gone, and there was only the vague glimmer of reflected light to mark its passing.

"Is there anyone waiting for you?" Raven asked.

"Waiting?"

Janna's confusion told Raven more than he had asked. She lived alone, as he did, and she had lived that way for so long that the idea of people worrying about her absence simply didn't occur to her.

"A husband, a lover, family, friends," he said softly, searching gray-green eyes. "Anyone who might be worried about you being out in a small boat in a storm."

"Oh." Janna laughed lightly and shrugged. "No. I'm twenty-four and fancy-free. I haven't had a husband for years, never had kids at all, my friends don't expect me back in Seattle until September and my landlady doesn't care where I am as long as the rent is on time. She drinks, you see. I'm paid through August, so she's not going to worry if I never come back."

Raven didn't know which surprised him more, that Janna had been married or that she was utterly alone in the Queen Charlottes for the next few weeks.

"Are you on vacation?" he asked.

Janna shrugged again. "Sort of. I'm doing some line drawings for a friend's book on the Queen Charlottes. I've been trying for weeks to get to Totem Inlet, but something always happened."

"Something?"

"Rain, usually. Mist, a lot. Wind, too."

Raven smiled. "Welcome to the Queen Charlottes."

"Yeah. Welcome all to hell." Janna laughed, taking the bite out of her words.

Slowly laughter faded. For a moment her eyes seemed almost silver once more, passion and emotion shimmering just below the surface.

"I've never seen a more savage place," she said, "or one that is more beautiful. The islands are...elemental. Creation is very close to the surface here, almost close enough to touch." She hesitated, then added softly, "It's as though the Charlottes have a special understanding with time. Time comes to the islands and then divides around them and passes by on either side like the sea. Other places change, but not the Charlottes. They have always been like this, barely condensed out of the mists of creation. Here, time doesn't exist. Only creation and mist."

For the second time since Raven had seen Janna, his scalp tightened as a wave of awareness shivered through him. Other people had noted that the islands had a savage aura, but to those people savage had meant *backward*, *awkward*, *brutal*, *uncivilized*. They had been afraid of the islands' raw strength and mysterious core of timelessness. Janna wasn't, even though she had nearly died exploring it.

"Yes," Raven said softly. "I love these islands, too. I come to them to renew my own silences."

"And now you're saddled with a chatty tourist," Janna said, grimacing. "Sorry about that."

"No problem," he said. "You're a woman who understands silence. You won't disturb me."

Janna couldn't help wondering what it would take for a woman to disturb Raven. She had no doubt that it would take a woman rather than a man; her former husband had taught her to be very aware of the fact that there were men who dated and married women but who could only be sexually attracted to another man. Raven wasn't like that. She was sure of it.

With a hidden sigh, Janna decided that Raven was probably like most men, drawn to blondes who had big mysterious eyes and more curves than a mountain road. The old cliché about gentlemen preferring blondes was quite true. So did jocks, thugs, poets and nerds. Forget women with brown hair, no matter how great their sense of humor.

Nobody ever cared if a blonde had a sense of humor, great or otherwise.

"You never answered my question about breakfast," Raven said. He looked over his shoulder and checked the progress of the water heating in a kettle on the small galley stove that was just across the aisle from his bunk. "Are you hungry?"

"Are you kidding? That isn't thunder you're hearing, it's my stomach," she announced, waving her hand dramatically, only to have to make a wild grab for the drifting blanket.

Raven glanced away quickly, not wanting Janna to realize that she had inadvertently shown him a firmly curved breast topped by a nipple that was such a velvety pink that he had to clench his hands against reaching toward her.

The teakettle whistled, offering Raven a much-needed distraction. He lifted the kettle and poured water into two mugs, wondering how Janna would react if he told her how perfect she had felt stretched out along his body. Soft. Resilient. No hard edges or angles. But if he said anything like that to her, it would sound like the opening gambit in a bid for sex. He knew that she didn't want that anymore. He had seen the desire fade from her after he had tucked in the blanket around her shoulders. The shimmering veils of passionate emotion had gone as though they had never existed, leaving only laughter in her clear gray-green eyes.

He wondered why that made him feel both sad and very angry, as though he should have taken what she had offered when she had offered it and not had any scruples about why she wanted him. Other women had wanted or not wanted him, and it hadn't mattered in any real way. Except for Angel. Her rejection had made pain a part of his everyday life. Finally, long before Miles Hawkins had met Angel, Raven had understood that some things were not meant to be. For him, Angel was one of them. He could either accept that, or he could destroy himself over it.

In the end, he had accepted it as he accepted storms and elusive fish and the powerful body that made men and women nervous. Life was what it was. He was what he was. Love was what it was.

Beyond his reach.

# Chapter 3

"Do you have a knife?" muttered Janna.

Raven heard the disgust in her muffled voice. Beneath his black mustache, his lips shifted into a smile at the picture she made. She was kneeling over the freshwater creek and wringing out her soapy hair. The long, curving lines of her body were revealed through the water-splashed flannel of one of his shirts. Below the trailing ends of cloth, her calves were pale and smooth, tautly curved, glowing in the misty light that was characteristic of the Queen Charlottes.

"Yes," Raven mumbled. "I have a knife."

"Good. Cut off this mess, would you?"

"I have a better idea."

"Shaving it off?" she retorted. "Sold!"

Janna felt as much as heard Raven's laughter when he knelt next to her on the moss-covered ground. His chest rubbed against her back as his fingers slid into the soapy, slippery mass of her hair.

"I didn't mean that you had to wash my hair."

"Your arm is still sore, isn't it? Rest. I'll take care of it."

"I've done nothing but lie around and let you take care of me since you fished me out of the inlet," Janna protested.

"A whole thirty hours," Raven said gravely. "Such laziness. I'll have to report you to the tourist bureau."

"But—"

"Hush," rumbled Raven. "I love a woman's long hair. Let me play with it."

Janna couldn't have answered if her life had depended on it. She was too caught up in the feel of Raven's big, gentle hands massaging her scalp. Chills went shivering over her flesh in response.

"Are you cold?" he asked, concerned. To him the day wasn't chilly, despite the wind that blustered and shredded clouds into sudden bursts of rain.

"I'm fine," Janna said quickly, suppressing another shiver. And it was true. She wasn't cold despite the fact that she was wearing only two layers of clothes—both of them Raven's. The soft cotton T-shirt held in her body heat and the heavy flannel shirt turned aside the occasional gusts of wind that reached the forest floor. It was Raven's touch that made her shiver, not the temperature.

"I'll hurry," he said.

Janna caught herself just before she told Raven to take his time, that she hadn't shivered because she was cold. In the end she said nothing, because she was afraid to open her mouth. If she did, she would probably whimper from the sheer pleasure of feeling his hands so strong and gentle as he washed her hair.

*Your brains really must be at the bottom of the inlet,* she told herself in disgust.

Her brains, yes. Her nerve endings, no.

*Think of Raven as one of your brothers.*

Janna tried to take her own excellent advice. It didn't work. The only times her brothers had had their hands in her hair was to give it a good yank. Never had they massaged her scalp with strong, slow, sensual motions.

*So think of Raven as your hairdresser. He has his hands in your hair all the time.*

Janna tried to think of Raven as her hairdresser. It was impossible.

Raven was…Raven. He was the most intriguing man she had ever met. Beneath his rough exterior he was a man capable of tenderness, laughter and the kind of silence that made her feel peaceful rather than uneasy.

And in him there was a promise of male sensuality that sent tiny streamers of fire through her. It should have frightened her. *He* should have frightened her. She hadn't been attracted to anyone since her divorce. She had been too vulnerable, too uncertain. Too afraid. Despite the assurances of her family and Mark's family, that none of it had been her fault, she still had the deep, never-spoken belief that if she had somehow been more of a woman, Mark would have been more of a man. It had taken almost two years before she could look in the mirror without silently asking herself if she had been bigger or smaller, lighter or darker, fatter or skinnier, Mark wouldn't have somehow been more attracted physically to her.

She had just gotten to the point where she could see herself in the mirror as a woman who might sexually interest a man, when she had found herself upside down and sinking fast in a cold sea. She had awakened naked in the arms of a man who was also naked. In short, she had had the best chance to attract Raven that any woman ever could, and what had happened?

He had all but chucked her under the chin, that's what.

Janna bit her lip against the thought that maybe Mark and her family and Mark's family had been wrong. Maybe there was just something lacking in her when it came to arousing a man.

Pale, slender fingers dug into the moss until Janna's knuckles went white. She forced herself to stop thinking about Mark and the sad mistake of their marriage. It was in the past. All of it. Mark had accepted what he was and was not and had made a better future for himself. She had to do the same.

Streamers of cool lather fell softly into the creek and dissolved immediately, vanishing. The lather that stayed behind on Janna's face was equally biodegradable, but it was running in the wrong direction. She swiped ineffectually at her cheek, angry at herself for fighting battles of self-esteem that she thought she had won or, at the very least, had stopped fighting herself over. She had a lot to offer a man. She could talk intelligently, cook very well, clean well enough, and identify things that crawled and swam on beaches all over the world. She was healthy, had all her own teeth, loved children and animals—and she had a great sense of humor.

Why did that list of virtues sound so depressing?

Janna sighed and squirmed unconsciously, as though trying to get away from her own thoughts.

"Hold still or you'll get soap in your eyes."

"How would I know the difference?" she mumbled, swiping at her face again.

"Sorry," Raven mumbled. "Guess I should have

kept my clumsy paws out of it. You were doing fine without me."

He started to ease his fingers from the sudsy mass of Janna's hair, only to have her grab his wrists, holding him in place.

"Don't stop," she said. "Please. It feels wonderful," she said, turning her face toward Raven. It was a mistake. The weathered tan of his skin, the slashing black lines of mustache and eyebrows, and the endless mystery of his eyes all sank into her like a series of blows that took her breath away. She drew air in raggedly and tried to explain to him what she didn't understand herself. "I don't know why I'm being so snarky. I guess my usual good nature got left out in the inlet along with my brains. I'm sorry."

Raven looked down at Janna's lather-streaked face and earnest, silver-green eyes. Her moist, slightly parted lips were the same raspberry color as the tip of her breast had been. The realization made heat and heaviness sweep through Raven's body, settling in the part of him that was even now nestled against her lovely, firm bottom. He wondered what it would feel like to be naked with her right now, his hands rubbing through her hair, sliding over her body, arousing her until she opened herself and cried for him to come to her.

Even as the thought swept through Raven, he denied it, ignored it, discarded it. He had spent too many years torturing himself over a woman he couldn't have. He wasn't going to start all over now, not even in the smallest way. Janna was here by accident, not by choice. Under normal circumstances she would never have agreed to stay in the lonely inlet with a man who looked as rough as he did. Not if she had a choice. The storm had taken choice from her, stranding her with him in Totem Inlet's isolation. If he took advantage of that and of the grati-

tude that softened Janna's magnificent, silver-green eyes
when she looked at him, he would hate himself. As soon
as the storm broke, he would take her to Masset. They
would stand on the dock and shake hands and smile
rather uncomfortably as they parted, two people who
never would have met under normal circumstances.

"Raven?"

He smiled sadly, slid one hand from Janna's hair and
picked up a nearby towel. With immense gentleness he
held her still and wiped the lather from her face.

"Put this over your eyes while I rinse you off."

Janna wanted to protest as Raven covered her eyes
with the towel, but she didn't. She wanted to ask if it
was something she had done that had made him so sad,
but she wasn't going to do that, either. At least, she told
herself she wasn't going to, right up to the instant when
she heard her own words.

"Is something wrong?" she asked, staying Raven's
hand when he would have turned her.

"Nothing new," he said simply. "And nothing
wrong, really. Turn around. If you get soap in your
eyes, you'll cry."

"I feel like crying right now, and I never cry," Janna
said, searching Raven's midnight eyes.

His big, blunt fingertip touched her nose lightly.
"That's just the last echoes of the adrenaline from yesterday. It will pass."

Gently, implacably, Raven turned Janna away from
him. He stripped soap from her hair into the stream,
moving with swift economy, no longer lingering to
enjoy the sensual weight and texture of her hair in his
hands. He rinsed her hair first with cold water from the
creek, then finally with the bucket of water he had
warmed on the galley stove and carried to the stream.

Janna let out a long sigh. "That feels wonderful."

Raven smiled and continued to work the warm water through her hair, rinsing away the last traces of soap. As Janna's hair lay wet between his hands, it seemed almost sable, yet it gleamed with hints of mahogany and gold. He wondered what her hair would look like in sunlight. Would the long strands be reddish brown or richly cinnamon? Would they be as straight as his own or they would curl seductively around his hands?

With a silent inward curse, Raven caught his glittering thoughts once again in the net of his will. He squeezed excess water from Janna's hair and began drying it with the towel. Her hair felt very soft, very clingy, and gleamed like wet silk in the stormy light.

"I can do that," Janna said, feeling guilty about causing Raven so much trouble. "You came here to be alone, not to be a lady's maid."

Raven removed his hands from Janna's tempting hair and stood up in a surge of controlled strength. "I'll wait for you on the shore. Do you like clams?"

"Nope. I love clams. Different thing entirely."

Raven grinned suddenly. "Raw?"

Janna stopped rubbing her hair with the towel and looked up. Her face was flushed from bending over the creek. Her eyes had the brilliance of sun-shot mist. "Raw clams?" she asked carefully, wondering if she had understood him. She loved clams, but had never brought herself to eat them raw.

"Umm," he said.

"Is that a rumble-yes or a rumble-no?" she retorted.

Raven laughed. "Just a rumble. How about clam chowder with raw oysters on the side?"

"Sold," she said promptly, diving back into the towel,

trying to ignore how she had gone weak just looking at Raven's wicked smile. From the depths of the towel, she asked, "Are they any good raw?"

"Oysters?"

"Clams."

"Raw?" he asked innocently. "I don't know. Are they?"

"Good?"

"No. Raw."

Janna's hands stilled as she heard the laughter vibrating in Raven's voice. Surrounded by a cloud of flying hair, her face emerged from the towel. "Do you know my brothers by any chance? I used to have this conversation with them all the time."

"Was it good?"

"And raw!"

"Then they weren't clams." Raven's smile flashed whitely, changing his face from brooding to amused in a single instant.

"Oh, help," Janna groaned, diving back beneath the towel.

"Thought you wanted to do that yourself," he said, reaching for the towel once more.

Janna's answer was muffled beneath strategically placed folds of towel. Raven's laugh wasn't. By the time he finished with her hair, she was laughing, too. She stood patiently while he combed out tangles with a gentleness that kept surprising her in a man of his size. In his broad hand the comb looked like a half-scale toy. It seemed impossible that such a powerful man could have such precise control of his every motion.

"Braid?" he asked.

"If I do, it will never dry. Sure you won't let me use your knife?"

"Positive. How about blow-drying it instead?"

"Sure. And a manicure, too, while you're at it," she retorted wryly, thinking Raven was teasing her again.

"Don't know about the nail polish. Angel never used it."

The way Raven's voice softened as he said the word Angel told Janna more than she wanted to know.

"I take it that this Angel is of the wingless, two-legged, earthbound variety?" Janna asked lightly.

He smiled. "So she keeps telling me. Never believed her, myself." He smoothed his palm over Janna's hair. "I should have thought of it yesterday."

"You were too busy rescuing me to think of angels."

"I meant the box."

"Help."

Raven tugged very gently at a damp stand of hair. "Quit teasing me. Angel left some stuff on the boat last summer. I'd forgotten about it until I saw your hair shining beneath my hand."

Silently Janna wondered if Angel was a summer resident like herself, here today and gone in September. Had Raven loved Angel only to lose her at the end of the summer? Was Angel coming back? Was that why she had left a box of things on his boat?

Was that why Raven wasn't attracted to Janna?

Janna bit her lip against the words crowding her tongue. If Raven wanted her to know about his Angel, he would tell her without being prodded by unsubtle questions such as: *Were you married to her? Are you married still? Are you in love? Engaged? Who are you, Carlson Raven? Why does your sadness and your laughter tear at me until I want to cry and laugh, too?*

Janna watched as Raven bent down, loaded shampoo and other items into the bucket and turned toward her. Every movement was both enormously powerful and oddly beautiful. It was like watching the tide flowing, strength both smooth and endless, supple and potent. She had been raised among big men, strong men; male strength had always thwarted and irritated her, not fascinated her. But Raven was different. She could not stop watching him.

"Ready?" Raven asked, holding the wire-handled bucket in one big hand.

Silently Janna turned and walked from the creek through a screen of windswept, mist-spangled cedar to the rocky margin where sea met land. The path she followed was overgrown, barely visible, older than the thick evergreens lifting to the sky. She wondered if Raven's people had come from the abandoned village whose rough-hewn cedar houses and savage totems were slowly being engulfed by the resurgent forest. Had his ancestors carved the eerie, powerful images that faced the sea like human cries frozen within time?

"Careful," Raven said, clutching Janna as she stumbled on a mossy rock. "We're going to have to tie up your socks."

Janna felt Raven's breathtaking, casual strength as he steadied and then released her. She looked down at her feet. Her tennis shoes had survived their dip in the inlet and their subsequent drying in the galley oven, but her socks had been kicked aside and forgotten in Raven's haste to warm her. As a result, today she was wearing a pair of his wool socks while hers decorated the galley railing. She had rolled and rolled the borrowed socks, but the heel still came above her ankle. It was the same for her shirt. Raven's shirt, actually. The cuffs engulfed her entire hand and the tail came below her knees.

With a sigh, Janna conceded that the islands had reduced her to looking like a refugee from a low-budget circus. All she needed was thick makeup and a painted-on smile.

Watching Raven didn't make her feel any better about her own appearance. He looked as elemental as the land itself. Wind and wet cedar boughs had combed his hair into an untamed black pelt that gleamed darkly with every shift of his body. It was the same for the rest of him; he was perfectly suited to the place and the time, as though he had always been here, a part of the island's savage perfection. She was a ragged urchin—and he was the mist and the rugged mountains, the wind and the wild sea. It was there in his fathomless eyes, in his immense strength, in his silences.

Shivering with reaction to Raven's elemental presence, Janna rubbed her hands up and down her arms. The knowledge that Raven had worn the very shirt that was warming her flesh didn't soothe her. Nothing about him soothed her. Yet even as that thought came, she knew it wasn't completely true. Nothing in her life had ever felt as right as the instants before she fell asleep with his powerful arms around her and his big body radiating heat into her own chilled flesh. She had never felt safer, more at peace, more cherished.

Raven looked back over his shoulder in time to see Janna shiver and rub her arms as though trying to warm herself. He frowned, wondering if she were coming down with a fever. He held aside the last evergreen barrier between himself and the beach and motioned Janna forward. As she brushed by him he looked intently at her. Other than the subtle sadness that came over her face at times, there was nothing obviously wrong with her. Her skin didn't look dry or pale.

"Wait," Raven said, releasing the cedar bough.

Janna turned. "Is something—"

Her breath hissed in as he put one hand on her shoulder and the other on her forehead. The fragrance of evergreen clinging to him teased her nostrils. She knew that she would never smell cedar again without remembering this instant, Raven so close to her that she couldn't take a breath without drawing in his scent, primal man and evergreen combined.

"You were shivering," he said, his voice rumbling gently. "You feel fine, though. No fever."

*That won't last if you keep touching me.*

Janna crushed her thought before it became incautious words. She had learned with her husband that if a man didn't want you, he didn't want you. Period. She had read an entire shelf full of books whose sexual instructions were both explicit and frankly boggling. She had gritted her teeth, taken a deep breath and tried some of those "surefire" methods of arousal on Mark.

It had been about as arousing as a bucket of ice water. For both of them.

"I'm fine," Janna said with determined cheerfulness, stepping away from Raven's touch before she shivered again in response to his closeness. "Actually, I'm disgustingly healthy. No feminine fits of the vapors, no delicate squeamishness, no interesting pallor. Just hearty, wholesome American girl. All I need are gingham checks, patent shoes and a puppy dog pulling at my anklets."

Raven heard the unhappiness underlying Janna's wry words. He looked intently at her, wondering what had happened to her that she so underestimated her own appeal to men. It would take a blind man not to respond to her. Her hair was a silky wildness framing her oval face. The forest green of his flannel shirt made her skin glow like mother-of-pearl on a sunrise beach. Her eyes picked up the green of cloth and forest, changing it, silvering it with emotions the way the wind changed the surface of the sea. Even the oversize shirt couldn't hide the womanly promise of her breasts, the allure of hip and thigh, the feminine curves leading down to ankles that looked ridiculously slender rising out of his bunched socks.

Watching Janna as she stood framed against the ancient forest made Raven want to smooth away all the coarse masculine clothes, to brush her with satin and incense, to caress the essential femininity of her. He wanted to arouse her until she cried out his name and wept and left passionate marks on his body. He wanted to give her a pleasure to equal the courage and determination he had seen when she had pushed herself beyond exhaustion, driven by the bitter imperatives of survival, and, then, still in the grip of those imperatives, she had let go of fighting and given herself to him, trusting him as no one ever had, even Angel.

Emotion went through Raven like a gust of wind through the cedar forest, stirring everything, leaving restlessness in its wake. Through narrowed eyes he watched as Janna picked her way over slippery rocks toward the log he had lashed to old, rotted cedar posts jutting up from the beach. The makeshift dock bobbed unpredictably. Years ago he had been a logger; for him, the erratic motions of a log floating on water were as easy to walk on as a stairway. Janna, however, lacked the experience to know how the log would react to a push here and a nudge there. Several times she had almost come to grief.

Janna stood on the shore, eyeing the bobbing log distrustfully. She tested the dampness of her hair, hesitated and shrugged.

"It's not worth it," she muttered, turning away.

"What isn't?"

"Dry hair. I'll slip on that log and take a header into the inlet," she said in a resigned tone. She shivered again. This time it was the wind off the inlet rather than Raven's presence that drew the involuntary response. "On second thought, it's worth it for the jeans alone. If they're dry by now?" she added, looking up at Raven.

"Should be."

"I was afraid you'd say that."

"Wait," Raven said, touching Janna's arm. "I'll get your jeans for you. And a scarf," he added as the wind lifted her hair in a damp, silky cloud. A few of the flying auburn strands caressed his face. They felt cool and smelled sweet against the tangy, salt-laden wind.

"Afraid you'll have to fish me out again?" Janna asked wryly, eyeing the log.

Raven felt his body kindle at the memory of drying Janna off and wrapping her in a warm blanket. Naked. With a muffled sound of exasperation at his unruly thoughts, he walked the log to the *Black Star*. Moments later he returned with her jeans, still warm from the oven, and a scarf that was the clear blue-green color of the sea under full sunlight. Janna took one look at the fine, delicate cloth and knew that it was Angel's.

"No," Janna said, refusing the scarf. "I'll ruin it." She stared at the glorious, blue-green wisp and had a depressing thought. "I'll bet it's the same color as her eyes."

Raven's black eyebrows shot up. "How did you know?"

Janna sighed. "She's blond, too. Right? Small boned, willowy, graceful, a figure to break your heart, with a smile that hints at passion and tragedy?"

"Are you a witch?" he asked, only half joking.

"If I were, Angel would be a warthog," Janna muttered under her breath.

"What?"

"Nothing," she said brightly.

Janna glared at her jeans and looked around for a place to sit that wasn't wet. The closest one was on the boat. She muttered one of her brothers' favorite words. Life simply wasn't fair. In order to put on her jeans without getting wet, she was going to have to hop around on one foot and then the other, looking about as graceful as a pig on roller skates. Meanwhile Raven could watch and compare her with the oh-so-delicate Angel.

Mentally Janna sorted through her brothers' vocabulary of locker-room epithets. She found some truly appalling phrases and spoke them in the silence of her mind. Finally she smiled, feeling better. She'd always known her brothers were good for something.

"Here," Raven said, realizing Janna's difficulty as she tried to balance on one foot on the slick pebble beach. "Brace yourself against me."

She hesitated, then mentally shrugged. He'd had her naked in bed and hadn't turned a hair. He was hardly going to be affected if she braced her fanny against his thighs while she put the jeans on in the only way possible to mortals—one leg at a time.

Leaning against Raven wasn't quite enough to make the job easy. The jeans were a little overcooked; they had shrunk in the oven. Now they fit her the way bark fit a tree—faithful to even the tiniest curve and hollow. Wriggling into the stubborn cloth was the only way to get the jeans on. With her tennis shoes catching every inch of the way, she had to do some major wriggling to get the jeans up her legs.

Raven suffered the innocent bump and grind of Janna's sexy bottom against his thighs as long as he could before he slipped an arm around her rib cage and braced her firmly, hoping that she would have to squirm around less that way. The strategy was partially successful. She did indeed have to squirm less. On the other hand, her breasts inevitably rested on his forearm, their sweet weight swaying with every movement of her body. Raven didn't know whether to regret or applaud the fact that Janna's bra, like her socks, had been lost in the first frantic moments of undressing her and getting her warm.

He remembered finding the bra that morning. The sheer midnight-blue lace had looked incredibly fragile in his hand. The thought of undressing her again had come to him like lightning; only this time it would be the heat of his tongue that transformed her nipples into tight pink crowns. He could almost see them pushing against the delicate lace, rising to the caress of his mouth.

The sensual images glittered through Raven's mind, impossible to control, like salmon schooling in the sea's mysterious darkness, gathering for the freshwater culmination that sang to them from their deepest instincts.

With a barely stifled groan Raven turned, using his hip to brace Janna rather than his thighs. The speed and intensity of his arousal surprised him. He told himself forcefully that he was no boy to go crazy over a woman's unconfined breasts brushing against his arm. He had solved the sexual mystery of male and female long ago. He knew his own needs, knew when to control them and when to appease them. Now was definitely not the time for appeasing.

In the most primitive analysis, Janna was helpless against him—and they both knew it. He was far stronger. He knew the land, knew the sea, knew how to survive on both. He had saved her life. She was utterly dependent on the civilized veneer that covered his elemental survival calculations. She knew that, too, at some unconscious, primitive level far deeper than language and culture.

And she was too damned vulnerable because of it. If he asked, she would give herself to him. He could see it in her eyes as she watched him almost secretly—admiration to the point of hero-worship. Or was it simply fear? Was that why she sometimes trembled when she brushed against him? Had she instinctively sensed what he had only just realized?

He wanted her with an intensity that bordered on violence.

He had wanted her since he had seen her refusal to give in against overwhelming odds. He had saved her life, and now some savage, ungovernable part of his mind insisted that she was his for the taking.

Even as the realization came he fought against it. He didn't want her like that, a woman coming to him for all the wrong reasons, gratitude and a primitive survival reflex driving her into his arms. He wanted Janna to come to him willingly, when she had all the alternatives of civilization open before her.

And if he kept telling himself that often enough, he might even believe it.

# Chapter 4

The tide was out, leaving behind a damp, plant-slicked, glistening swath of shoreline for Raven and Janna to pick over in their search for dinner. Living off the land wasn't really necessary; Raven had enough emergency stores to keep both himself and Janna well fed for the days it would take for the storm to blow itself out along the coast. On the other hand, he was reluctant to use the emergency food unless he had to. Though the chance of the storm lasting more than a few days was small, it was on such small chances that survival often hinged. More people got into trouble through bad planning than bad luck.

Besides, Raven very much enjoyed walking along the shoreline with Janna in search of food. It was the time between squall lines, when the rain was little more than a sparkling edge to the wind. Janna accepted the wind and mist and rain with the same good nature she accepted having to wear sweaters and jackets that came down to her knees.

Raven could think of a lot of women who would have shut themselves up in the warm boat rather than scramble over chilly, slippery rocks in search of seashore life that only a scientist or a very hungry person could describe in terms of enthusiasm. Janna was both. She was happily crouched over a stretch of rocky tide pools that waves would bury in foam within a few hours. Slick seaweed glistened around her. Beneath the oversize jacket she wore, her legs looked very sleek and feminine encased in her jeans. Raven knew that her legs would look even better on the boat, when she would wear nothing more than one of his long shirts while her jeans toasted and dried in the oven.

The thought made Raven smile. He knew he would never again be able to smell sea-wet jeans and tennis shoes drying without remembering the days when a summer storm had given him a gift and then sealed him within Totem Inlet to enjoy the present. Raven couldn't think of a time he had had half so much fun as he had in the past three days. Janna was good company. Her quick mind and wry sense of humor had made the hours fly—at least in the daytime. Knowing that she was only a few feet away had made the nights incredibly long.

"What do you call this?" Janna asked, turning toward Raven.

He stared from the creature balanced on the palm of her hand to Janna, disbelief clear on his rugged face. "What did you say you majored in?"

Janna blinked, then began laughing. "Marine biology. If it will make you feel better, I know that what I'm holding is phylum Echinodermata, class Echinoidea,

and is known to its friends as *Strongylocentrotus pur-
puratus*. Now, what do you call it?"

"A purple sea urchin," Raven said dryly.

Janna looked up at the cloudy, windswept, glittering
sky as though seeking aid or inspiration. "In Haida," she
said carefully. "What do you call a purple sea urchin in
Haida?"

Janna turned her face back to Raven, waiting for him
to speak. Her head was cocked in an attitude of anticipation. She had learned from him that the Haida
language was technically described as an isolate, a
language totally unrelated to any other on the face of
the earth. Basque was the only other living language
that was an isolate. All other spoken languages
belonged to one or another inter-related groups, such as
the Romance languages. But not Haida. It stood alone,
isolated. Unique.

Like Raven, who also fascinated her.

Raven's lips quirked as he measured Janna's eager-
ness. He was oddly proud that the Haida language truly
intrigued her. He had always known that his native
speech was different, but through Janna's eyes he was
learning just how rare his language really was. Learning
like that was an unusual experience. So was Janna. With
her around life grew more interesting with every instant.

"Raven?"

He laughed softly before he answered her question
in Haida.

Janna listened to the brief rumble of sound that was
the Haida name for the purple sea urchin. "What does
it mean?" she asked.

Beneath the gleaming midnight mustache, Raven
smiled widely. "There's no—"

"Direct translation," interrupted Janna, groaning. It

was a phrase she had heard too many times lately. "So give me an indirect one."

"Round, purple, spiny, edible, sea-rock dweller."

"See?" Janna demanded triumphantly. "No matter how unique the language, the human mind that thought it up is still wired along the same basic diagram. Descriptive. The scientific name for purple urchins tells me pretty much the same thing as the Haida name, but in more detail. Except for edible." She grinned. "Most scientists aren't interested in eating the subjects of their studies."

Raven eyed the prickly, violently purple urchin that Janna held. "I know how they feel," he said emphatically. "Takes your appetite away just to look at it."

"In Japan, the roe of the urchin is a delicacy, like caviar in Russia."

"We aren't in Japan."

"Where's your sense of adventure?"

"In the bottom of the inlet along with your brains," Raven retorted.

"No urchin soup?"

"No urchin soup."

"How about raw urchin?"

"How about raw sand?"

"Eagles eat urchins," Janna pointed out, remembering her surprise when she had seen an immature bald eagle perched on a log and eating an urchin with every evidence of enjoyment.

"My moiety is raven, not eagle."

The teasing light vanished from Janna's eyes, to be replaced by a curiosity that was much more intense. She wanted—she *needed*—to know everything about Raven. "What?"

"Haidas are divided into two groups, eagle and

raven," he explained. "My mother was a raven. Therefore, I'm a raven."

"The Haidas have a matriarchal society?"

"In some ways." He smiled crookedly. "It's just as
well, since my father was a Scots sport fisherman
named Carl who left as soon as the salmon run was over.
So I'm Carlson Raven."

"Did he know your mother was pregnant?" asked
Janna. Even as the words left her mouth, she knew that
her curiosity was almost rude, but she couldn't help
herself. She needed to know more about Raven with an
urgency that overrode her polite upbringing.

"I doubt it," Raven said, shrugging. "And I doubt that
it would have mattered if he had known." Raven hesitated, then added quietly, "He picked my mother up in
a bar. She never had enough money to buy all the drinks
she wanted."

Janna's eyes became even more silver as a sheen of
tears unexpectedly gathered. She thought of how proud
her father had been of his strong sons and lively
daughter, and of how much love there had been between
herself and her family. Then she thought of Raven
growing up without that kind of love.

"What a waste," she whispered. "Most men would kill
to have a son like you, and most women would die proud
knowing that they had once carried you in their body."

For an instant Raven closed his eyes, unable to bear
the depth of emotion he saw in Janna's. "Not really," he
said finally, his voice almost harsh. His eyes opened
black and very clear. "I'm Haida. Indian. Maybe that
doesn't matter here and now in this inlet, but it matters
like hell out there," he said flatly, gesturing with a broad,
powerful hand to the rest of the world.

Janna started to object, then stopped. What Raven

said was true. She didn't like it, but she was too realistic to deny it. She hated it, though. She hated it so intensely that her eyes became almost as dark as his. The thought of Raven being subjected to a loveless childhood and then to bigotry in adulthood made her so angry that she shook with the force of her suppressed emotion.

"I don't feel that way about you," she said distinctly. "You're a man, Carlson Raven. You're as fine a man as I've ever met. That's all that matters to me. That won't change whether I'm here in Totem Inlet or on the far side of the moon. And I can't bear the thought of you being raised without love, without someone to appreciate what you've become."

Janna's voice broke. She turned away quickly, replacing the spiky, fragile urchin in its nest of stone. Impatiently she wiped off her tears on the thick sweater that she wore. It was damp and smelled subtly of the sea and the man who had worn it before he had given it to her to keep her warm.

"Janna." Raven's voice was deep, gentle, gritty with restraint.

He pulled her to her feet and put his work-hardened palm beneath her chin, tilting her face up to his. He started to speak, saw her tears and felt breath rush out of his lungs as though at a blow. He bent and brushed her eyelashes with his lips. The effort it took to stop after those comforting, undemanding kisses shocked him. Slowly he released her chin, caressing the line of her jaw with his fingertips as he withdrew his hand.

"I wasn't unhappy," he said softly. "Among the Haida, children belong to their mother's moiety, and boys are initiated by their mother's brothers rather than by their fathers. My uncle raised me, as is the custom among my people."

"And your mother?" Janna asked unevenly, knowing that she shouldn't ask...unable to stop herself.

"By the time I was six my mother wasn't capable of caring for herself, much less for a son. She abandoned me and took up full-time drinking. My uncle adopted me under both tribal and Canadian law four years before she died. Eddy is a good man, a strong man, a kind man," Raven said deeply. "In the summer he fishes salmon and in the winter he carves argillite into images as old and unique as the Haida language. You'd like Eddy. He would love you. He has nothing but disgust for women who are too spoiled to walk the Queen Charlottes in a storm."

Janna looked intently at Raven, measuring the emotion that lay beneath his words. She sensed that he didn't talk casually about his parents—or lack of them—yet he had talked to her. As she looked up into his black, gleaming eyes, it was all she could do not to throw herself into Raven's arms and plead that he notice her as a woman. But throwing herself at him would be a disaster. Whatever Eddy might like, Raven himself was drawn to tragic, fragile blondes who wore silk scarves that exactly matched their mysterious blue-green eyes.

"Do you think Eddy's man enough to eat urchin soup?" Janna asked lightly, hoping Raven wouldn't notice that her smile quivered on the edge of turning upside down.

Raven smiled suddenly, transforming the dark, harsh planes of his face. "I can't wait to find out."

When Janna saw Raven's smile, emotion gusted over her like wind over the surface of the sea. She turned quickly and looked out at the water. Another squall line was sweeping in. "How long do we have to wait?" she asked.

"For the soup?"

"For the squall."

Raven's glance followed hers. He frowned as he saw the dense, blue-black wall of clouds advancing toward them on the back of a freshening wind. "Just long enough to get to the boat, if we're lucky. *Damn*. What the hell was I thinking of? I know better than to turn my back on the sea."

"No time for oysters?" asked Janna, thinking of the small oyster bed they had passed on their way to the mouth of the inlet.

"I'll get some. You go on to the boat and stay dry."

"What about you?"

"Getting wet will teach me to keep my mind on the weather." *And off how sexy your hips look when you bend over and sort through the contents of a tide pool,* Raven added silently.

"But you'll run out of dry clothes," Janna said.

"I'll wear a sleeping bag."

"No way," she said, shaking her head firmly, making light flicker and run through her softly curling cinnamon hair. "I'll wear a sheet and give you back your own clothes."

The thought of Janna naked but for a dark blue sheet made Raven smile despite his promises to himself not to think of her in any way except as a friend or a sister.

Janna didn't see the very male smile because she had already turned and started up the shore toward the part of the inlet where the *Black Star* was moored. Raven watched her for a few moments, admiring the quintessentially feminine swing of her hips. With a muffled curse he admitted to himself how much he itched to trace Janna's graceful spine and the smooth, full curves of her bottom with his tongue and fingertips. She would feel so good, warm and firm, soft and womanly, filling his senses even as he filled her. Would she like that? Would she like being teased and tasted and finally taken by him?

The direction of Raven's thoughts was rapidly making walking uncomfortable for him. Cursing silently, he wondered how he was going to keep his hands off her for the two more days of rain and wind that the storm was predicted to run.

"Raven?" called Janna.

He looked up and realized that he had stopped walking while he fought his unruly thoughts and hungry body. Furiously he swore beneath his breath. Self-control had never been this much of a problem for him, even when he had been a boy in the first raw rush of sexuality.

"Is something wrong?" Janna asked.

"No," he said, his voice almost harsh. "I was just wondering how much longer we'll be shut up in this damned inlet."

"Oh."

Janna smiled brightly, meaninglessly. She turned and walked away from Raven as quickly as possible, all the pleasure gone from her day. She had been enjoying every instant of being marooned with Raven. It was deflating to realize that he was counting the minutes until the storm let up enough to permit them to leave. Deflating, but not surprising. If he had ever fantasized about being trapped in a deserted inlet, it would be Angel who filled his dreams, not a strange brunette with an off-the-wall sense of humor.

Raven, on the other hand, was the kind of man Janna had dreamed about long before he had fished her from the cold sea. His intelligence appealed to her as much as his strength, and his laughter made her feel as though she had stepped into a cataract of sunlight. The thought of being wanted by a man like that—really *desired*— made her tremble.

The squall line came ashore just as Janna scrambled into the boat's cabin. The second log that Raven had lashed to the original mooring log made it easier for her to walk along the bobbing "dock" to the boat without slipping. Even so, she was grateful that she wouldn't have to attempt crossing the erratically moving surface in the rain.

She smiled almost sadly. It had been very thoughtful of Raven to round up another one of the old, weathered logs that lined the inlet and add it to the "dock" just so that she wouldn't risk a dunking every time she came or went from the boat. She had watched in fascination as he stripped to his waist and maneuvered the log into the water. The raw strength of Raven's body had been almost frightening.

Yet she had wanted nothing more than to run her hands over that powerful flesh, savoring the male heat and strength, the textures both smooth and intriguingly furry. She wondered if his sweat would taste like the sea or would have the astringency of cedar. Or perhaps his taste would be a blend of salt and evergreen and man, a mixture as complex and elemental as Raven himself.

"He could taste like caviar and cherry pie for all you know or will know," Janna muttered to herself. "Or lightning and rain, or wine and—oh, the hell with it. Stop torturing yourself over what you can't have and make some tea. He's going to be wet and cold by the time he gathers a bucket of oysters for dinner."

While the water heated Janna put out two mugs, each with its own tea infuser. She liked her tea fairly mild,

with lemon peel and sugar. Raven liked his tea strong
enough to etch steel. Then he added canned milk and
sugar in the British fashion. Janna had tried it. She still
wasn't sure what it had tasted like. She knew what it had
not tasted like, though. Tea.

As soon as the water boiled she poured it into the
mugs, carefully leaving enough room in one for the
generous amount of milk Raven would add. She stepped
across the narrow galley aisle and sat at the custom-
made dining table that filled one side of the small cabin.
The table was larger than most ship's tables because
Raven was larger than most men. At night the table was
lowered, fitted into a groove and covered with a custom-
made mattress. Normally Raven simply left the bunk
made up and ate his meals sitting on one of the padded
seats in the stern of the boat. Since Janna had joined
him, he had insisted on setting up the table every
morning and taking it down after dinner every night.

Janna looked toward the small triangular cabin in the
bow of the boat where she slept. There was a narrow
bunk running down either side, leaving a wedge-shaped
aisle in between. One look at the bunks had told her why
Raven didn't sleep there. He would have hung over
everywhere. For her the bunk was quite comfortable.
For him it would have been a bad joke.

Absently Janna tested her tea by pulling out the
infuser and looking at the color of the liquid running
back into the mug. Perfect. She cut off a bit of lemon
peel with a galley knife. It was lethally sharp, as were
all Raven's knives. She was grateful. Only a sharp knife
held by a skilled, strong hand would have been able to
slice through the tough fabric of the life vest that had
bound her to the sinking rowboat.

She shivered unconsciously and added a teaspoon of

sugar to her tea. Carefully she rewrapped the small piece of lemon that was all that Raven had had in his cooler. She had been grateful to find even that. Lemons on the Queen Charlotte Islands were a rare and exotic life-form.

Restlessly Janna looked around the boat. Her glance fell on the small writing tablet and pencil that Raven had found for her so that she could make sketches. Even as she reached for the pad, she decided against it. The ruled lines would distract her, which simply meant that she was too edgy to sketch.

She went out to the *Black Star*'s stern. The canopy was snapped in place, keeping off both wind and rain, making another cabin out of the stern of the boat. The sound of rain was continuous, relentless. Normally she found it soothing. Now she just wanted to hear Raven's voice. She leaned forward, staring through the clear plastic windows in the canopy. There was nothing to see but rain. It was coming down so hard that she could barely see the shore.

The boat rocked gently against the fenders protecting the hull from the logs. Janna closed her eyes. For a long time she listened to the rain and the wind and the restless sea. She was used to being alone, yet she was not used to being lonely. And that was how she felt right now. Lonely.

"Hello the *Black Star*! Oysters coming on board."

Janna felt warmth flood through her. Even as she told herself that she was a fool for letting her heart and her hopes race, she set aside her tea and rushed over to unzip a section of the canopy. A bucket emerged into the opening, followed shortly by Raven himself. He fastened the canopy again and then turned toward Janna. He was as wet as a seal despite his waterproof jacket.

He peeled off the jacket, shook it and hung it on a peg before he sniffed the air.

"Ahh," he rumbled, "my favorite dinner. Roast haunch of tennis shoes with a side order of baked jeans."

Laughter bubbled from Janna as though she were freshly opened champagne. Raven's whimsical sense of humor had been as unexpected and endearing to her as his gentleness. She held out her hand for the bucket, only to notice that it held a bottle of wine as well as oysters.

"You have, er, unusual oyster beds in the Charlottes," Janna observed, pulling out the wine bottle.

Raven grinned. "Old Haida secret."

"Someone must have let the French in on it, too," she retorted, reading the label. "How did you know I love Chardonnay?"

"Like I said," Raven answered, his voice muffled as he bent down to pull off his soaking shoes, "you look like a woman who enjoys her senses."

"What did you do to your hand?" Janna asked suddenly, setting aside the wine.

He looked at the back of his left hand. There were several thin lines of blood welling. "Barnacles," he said, shrugging. What he didn't say was that he had been thinking about Janna when he should have been thinking about what he was doing. "No big deal," he added, cleaning off the skin with a quick swipe of his tongue and then examining the shallow cuts.

"It could be a big deal if you don't take care of it," she said crisply. "Barnacle cuts are notorious for getting infected."

She went back to the galley and returned in a few moments with hot water and an antibiotic salve. Before Raven could object she took his hand and bathed it carefully. She bent over his hand and turned it toward the light. The cuts were shallow, clean and should heal quickly. There was really no reason to worry about them. She should let go of his hand and get back to the cabin.

But Janna could not let go. The temptation to raise Raven's broad hand to her lips and kiss away the minor hurt was almost overwhelming. All that prevented her was the knowledge that the intent of her kiss would be more sensual than healing, more hungry than comforting. Silently calling herself a hundred kinds of fool, she prolonged the contact by bathing his hand again, touching him in the only way that she could.

Raven sat motionlessly in the stern seat, savoring the gentle warmth of Janna's hands. Her hair had come loose from the clip she wore at the nape of her neck. Tendrils of rich cinnamon curled softly across her cheeks like darkly shimmering flames. In the subdued light her hair glowed with life. He wondered what it would feel like to have that cool, silky hair falling freely over his bare arm, his chest, his thighs. Then he wondered why he was tormenting himself over a woman he would not let himself touch.

Janna dried Raven's hand with the same gentle thoroughness with which she had bathed it. She smoothed antibiotic salve over the tiny wounds, taking her time about it, doing it twice. When there was no further excuse to touch Raven, she reluctantly released his hand.

"There you are. Nearly as good as new." She heard her own voice and knew that it was too husky, almost breathless.

"Thanks."

Raven flexed his hand to keep from reaching out

and burying his fingers in Janna's beautiful hair and pulling her mouth down to his. He wanted to tell her how much he had enjoyed having her concerned over his minor scrapes and having his big, work-roughened hand touched as though she cared if he were hurt even by such a small thing as barnacle cuts. Normally he disliked women who fussed over him, oohing and cooing over every tiny scrape. Janna was different. She had cared for him so quietly and deftly that she had left him feeling cherished rather than smothered.

"You should have children. You'd be a fine mother. Gentle hands and…" Raven's deep voice died into silence as he saw the sudden stiffening of Janna's body. She straightened and turned away from him so quickly that she almost stumbled. "Janna?"

"I forgot your tea," she said tightly. "It will be strong enough to dissolve steel by now."

"Sounds perfect to me," he rumbled, smiling.

There was no answer. Raven frowned, wondering what was wrong. Normally Janna enjoyed teasing him about the strength of the tea he drank, just as he enjoyed ribbing her about the "hot sugar water" that she preferred. He got up to follow her and demand to know what was wrong. In three longs steps he was in the cabin.

"Janna, what—"

"As your mother surrogate," she interrupted in clipped tones, "I feel compelled to point out that you're dripping all over the floor."

"Deck," he corrected her automatically, frowning. *"Deck."*

Raven's eyes narrowed as he took in the barely restrained anger radiating from Janna. He watched as she reached blindly into a drawer and brought out a punch for the can of condensed milk. She opened the can with a single savage stroke, spilling some of the thick, creamy fluid in the process. Carefully he reached past her, took the milk and metal punch, and set them beyond her reach.

"What's wrong?" he asked.

"Nothing." Janna heard her own cold word echo in the silence, watched a thread of milk spread thickly on the counter and hung on to the shreds of her self-control with every bit of willpower she possessed. "Sorry," she said finally. "Guess I'm like you."

"How so?"

"Wondering how much longer we'll be 'shut up in this damned inlet.'"

Hearing his own words repeated like that made Raven flinch. "I didn't mean that the way it sounded. I've enjoyed the time here. I can't remember ever laughing so much."

"Yeah, a regular dream come true for you," Janna said with a bright, empty smile. "You never had a mother and I'm great motherhood material. Pity you're too old for me to adopt. We could have a lifetime of laughs."

"Janna—"

"Here," she said, interrupting, setting Raven's tea within his reach. "Drink this before it eats through the mug. I'll open the oysters. You change out of those wet clothes before you get cold."

"Yes, Mother," Raven said dryly, reaching for the top button of his shirt.

Janna flinched as though she had been slapped. Raven's black eyes narrowed as he saw her reaction.

"I didn't mean that as an insult," he said evenly.

"What woman could be insulted by being told she was great mother material?" Janna asked in a flat tone.

Raven started to say something, hesitated and settled for unbuttoning his shirt. After he pulled on dry clothes and draped the wet ones over anything handy, he went out to the stern. The canopy kept out wind and rain, but did little to preserve the warmth that made the cabin cosy.

"Aren't you cold?" he asked, eyeing Janna's long, bare legs gleaming beneath the tails of one of his flannel shirts.

She shrugged and continued wrestling with an oyster. The knife she used was very short, triangular and deadly. There was no guard on the hilt. So far she had managed to avoid stabbing anything but the oysters.

"I'll do that," Raven said. "Get back in the cabin where it's warm."

"Yes, Daddy," she muttered, but she didn't give up the oyster that she was struggling with.

The idea of feeling fatherly toward Janna was so preposterous that Raven couldn't do anything but laugh.

After a moment Janna looked up and smiled. It wasn't her best smile but it was all she had at the moment. She still was raw from hearing Raven praise her nice, motherly attributes at the very instant when she had been all shivery just from touching him. The difference between their reactions to one another couldn't have been greater...or more discouraging.

"Sorry," she said. "Guess it's cabin fever."

"Or hunger," he rumbled, touching her lips with his fingertip.

Janna's eyes widened with shock. She wondered whether Raven had read her mind. "How did you know?" she whispered.

"No great trick," he said, grinning. "It's been five hours since lunch."

"Lunch?"

"Yeah. You remember—the meal that comes after breakfast and before dinner?"

"Oh, that lunch."

"Is there more than one?" he asked innocently.

"Of course," she retorted, rallying. "There's lunch and then there's getting lunched. Lately I've been lunched more often than I've eaten."

Raven opened his mouth, closed it and then began to laugh. "Has anyone ever told you that you have—"

"A great sense of humor?" interrupted Janna, opening the oyster with a vicious jab of the knife. "Yeah. As one of the all-time boring virtues, it ranks right up there with motherhood."

"Not to someone who never had a mother and who likes to laugh. They're gifts, Janna," he said quietly.

"Really?" she asked, picking up another oyster, avoiding Raven's eyes. "Too bad we're so far from the complaint counter. I'd exchange them for sex appeal."

Raven's jaw dropped in the instant before he told himself that Janna was kidding. He laughed, shaking his head, and wondered why a storm hadn't washed Janna into his life years ago.

Janna didn't find the idea of her being sexy nearly as amusing as Raven did. In fact, she discovered that her sense of humor on that subject had just run out.

"Here," Janna said, slapping the hilt of the oyster knife into Raven's broad palm. "I'll make the cocktail sauce. It's too cold out here for me."

Raven looked from the knife to the long, bare legs vanishing into the cabin. The door shut firmly. He looked back at the knife and wondered why he had the distinct feeling that Janna would have liked to stick it into him rather than an oyster.

# Chapter 5

By the time Janna had finished rummaging through the galley in order to find ketchup and horseradish, she had regained some of her normal common-sense outlook and with it her usually easygoing temperament. As she reminded herself, it wasn't Raven's fault that he was drawn to tragic blond angels. Nor was it his problem that she was finding it harder and harder to be close to him without touching him in a decidedly unangelic fashion.

And the storm just kept calling wildly over land and sea.

From what Janna had been able to understand between the bursts of static that had come whenever Raven tried to pick up a station on the radio, they had at least two more days in Totem Inlet before the wind died down enough to make the ocean safer for small craft.

Just two days. Surely she could keep her yearnings to herself and her sense of humor intact for a mere two days.

Gloomily Janna put out the box of oyster crackers she had found in the cupboard. After a moment of frowning at the innocent crackers, she decided to sort through the *Black Star*'s spare cooler. She knew there weren't any lemons in the small galley refrigerator, but she had high hopes for the storage cooler. She hadn't found a lemon there yet, but then she hadn't really looked, either. It wasn't the sort of thing you did on a whim.

The cooler was little more than a long, deep plastic container set below waterline and shaped to conform to the curve of the hull. A hinged section of the counter lifted to give access to the cooler. Janna lifted the lid and looked in. No lemons had grown there since the last time she had looked, but she could swear that she smelled fresh lemons beneath the pervasive odor of onions and oranges. She stared down into the darkness at the small bags crowding against each other. Getting to the bottom of the cooler was going to require a flashlight and an ability to hang her head down in an enclosed space while balancing her weight on the edge of the counter and bracing her feet at floor level on the opposite cabinet.

That was exactly what Janna was doing when Raven came into the cabin. The sight of her long, naked legs stretched diagonally across the aisle brought him to a complete stop. Muffled thumps came from the cooler as Janna shifted potatoes, onions, carrots, oranges and other durable fresh foods from one side of the cooler to the other in her quest for lemons.

Raven barely noticed the sounds. He was fighting to control the impulse to run his hands from Janna's ankles

to the smooth curve of her hips…and from there to let
his fingers slide into the shadowed feminine secrets he
knew were waiting.

It would be easy to do, a few seconds, no more, and
he could peel away the dark blue lace briefs that even
now peeked from the edge of the oversize shirt. Or he
could take longer. Much longer. He could learn every
smooth bit of Janna with his teeth and his tongue,
nuzzling closer to her secrets as he slowly, slowly, eased
the lacy briefs down her beautiful legs.

Raven's hands were actually reaching for Janna
before he realized it. "What the hell do you think you're
doing?" he muttered roughly to himself.

An answer floated up from below the counter.
"Looking for lemons."

"Lemons," he repeated thickly, watching his own
shirt climb higher and higher up Janna's body as she
wriggled backward up and out of the cooler's depths.
When he saw the sweet flex and shift of Janna's hips
beneath blue lace, his whole body tightened. "Oh God,"
he gritted.

He closed his eyes for a few seconds and tried to
control his own hunger. It didn't work. Desire poured
in red-hot torrents through his blood and pooled
urgently, rigidly, between his thighs.

"Lemons," Janna said, her voice becoming clearer
with each instant as she emerged from hanging upside
down in the cooler. "You know—something to sweeten
my disposition."

Raven laughed almost helplessly and then swore in
the same way, but silently. He had been expecting to
have a tense dinner with an angry woman and had
walked into the cabin to find Janna's sexy bottom
tempting him and her sense of humor restored. Now, if

he could just do something about the raw, hard desire that was riding him, they might get out of the inlet before he took her down onto his bunk and ate every sweet inch of her.

And then again, they might not, especially if he didn't stop watching her hips move. Now. Right now.

With a groan Raven forced himself to look away from the inviting curves of Janna's bottom. By memory alone he found a plate for the oysters and retreated to the stern, shutting the cabin door behind. Using great care he stacked oysters on the plate. When he looked over his shoulder through the cabin window, Janna was head down in the cooler again. Grimly he rearranged the mound of oysters on the plate. Three times.

"I found some!"

"Thank God," Raven said with real feeling, turning toward the cabin.

He opened the door and closed it, balancing the heavy oyster plate in one hand. One look told him he had come back a few seconds too soon. Janna was just now wriggling onto her feet. Her face was flushed and her hair was tousled from hanging upside down for the past few minutes.

And her shirt was bunched at her waist.

Janna noticed the cloth, too. As her hands were full of lemons, she restored the shirt to its proper place with a quick shimmy of her hips. The tantalizing motion made Raven groan.

"Raven?" She turned toward him. "What is it? Did you stab yourself with the oyster knife?"

*No, but only because I wasn't holding it. God, woman, there should be a law against movements like that.*

Raven had just enough control left to keep the

thought to himself. He took a deep breath—and smelled hot tennis shoes.

Janna smelled them at the same instant. She dumped the lemons in the sink, yanked open the oven door and pulled out her forgotten jeans and shoes. Raven set aside the oysters just in time to snag a pair of flying jeans before they wrapped around his face. Janna tossed the shoes from hand to hand, muttering to herself.

"If I'd known you were this hungry, I'd have tried for some cod," he said, examining the jeans with deadpan distaste.

"Who was it that I heard earlier singing paeans of praise to baked jeans?" retorted Janna, dropping the hot but otherwise unhurt shoes to the deck.

Raven chuckled and folded the rapidly cooling jeans. Janna saw his big hands linger almost caressingly on the worn cloth of the seat and shivered, wishing she were wearing the jeans.

"Talk about hot pants," she muttered.

"What?"

"Er, are they cool enough to wear?" she asked quickly.

"Are you cold?"

Janna opened her mouth, thought better of it, and said, "No you don't."

Raven gave her a slow, sideways look. "No I don't what?"

"Sucker me into another one of those open-ended free-association conversations."

Smiling, Raven sat on his heels and poked cautiously at the tennies. He looked up and said gravely, "Give 'em another ten minutes while we have oysters on the half shell. The shoes should be tender by then."

"Good idea."

Before his astonished eyes she tossed the shoes in the

oven, cranked the control up to high and slammed the oven door. She turned and began mixing cocktail sauce as though nothing had happened. He waited. And waited.

And waited.

Suddenly Raven's deep, warm laughter filled the cabin. He bent over, shut off the oven and whisked the shoes out.

"You'd have done it, wouldn't you?" he asked, still laughing.

"Damn straight," she assured him, fighting the smile that insisted on shaping her lips into an amused curve. "The first thing a little sister learns is to out-stubborn brothers who are bigger, stronger and tougher than she is."

"Small warrior," Raven murmured, touching the cinnamon fire of Janna's hair so lightly that she didn't feel it. "Did they torment you?"

Janna started to agree emphatically, then realized that it wasn't quite true. "Sometimes, but they loved me in their own way. And I was a little witch to them. Sometimes."

"But you loved them all the time," Raven said, watching the softness that memories brought to Janna's mouth.

"Yes," she whispered. "They always tried to protect me. They used to drive me crazy vetting my dates, sending some of the boys running and scaring the others so that they were afraid to hold my hand. The only one they would let near me was the boy next door. They liked Mark. He never came on strong."

Janna's smile slipped. If only they had known why Mark wasn't aggressive with their nubile little sister. But it wasn't fair to blame them. Mark hadn't known, either. Not really.

"Mark? Your husband?"

"Once. No more."

"Why?"

Janna's hands paused. With deliberate motions she scraped the cocktail sauce into a small, shallow bowl. "We were all wrong for each other."

"What do you mean?" Raven asked, sensing something more than the usual things that pulled marriages apart.

She hesitated, then shrugged again. "Mark saw me as a friend, a companion, a sister, sometimes even a mother. But not a lover." Janna's voice was even, but all the softness was gone from her face and memories. "Do you want your lemon in the cocktail sauce or on the side?"

Raven looked at Janna for a long moment, wanting to ask more questions about her and the man she had once loved enough to marry—a man who apparently hadn't loved her.

"On the side," he said finally, asking none of his questions because Janna's eyes were jade green, no passionate silver, no emotion turning in the depths, nothing to tell him whether she had been sad or happy or indifferent when her marriage had ended.

*A companion, a sister, a mother, not a lover.*

Raven winced inwardly. No wonder Janna had stiffened when he had praised her in terms of her gentle hands and smile. He wondered if she had wanted her husband as a lover rather than a child. Even as the question came, he knew the answer; she had wanted a lover and had gotten a child.

"Your husband must have been blind," Raven said flatly.

"How gallant of you to say so," Janna said. Her full lips formed a smile that was as emotionless as her eyes. "But unnecessary and untrue. Mark was a pilot. He had superb vision. Do you have a corkscrew for the wine?"

"Did you love him?"

"Of course not," she said. "I marry every man who asks me out more than twice."

"Janna…" Raven began.

"Corkscrew?" she asked, smiling at him again, a smile as cool as her voice. "My brothers showed me how to take out the cork just by hitting the bottom of the bottle with my hand, but I'm not as strong as they are. I bruise my palm every time. You'd be good at it, though. Strong and hard. Like them."

"Do you still love him?"

"Did anyone ever tell you to mind your own business?"

"Yes. Do you still love him?"

"Why does it matter to you?" Janna asked through clenched teeth, feeling her careful veneer of dispassion disintegrating.

"I won't let you waste your life looking over your shoulder," Raven said quietly.

"You won't let me." Janna's teeth clicked as she shut her mouth and stared at the big, immovable man in front of her. "You aren't responsible for my life. I already have a father and three older brothers who are almost as big and every bit as overbearing as you."

"Do you still love Mark?" Raven asked relentlessly.

"No! I haven't loved him since he cried himself to sleep in my arms because he couldn't bring himself to have sex with me!"

*"What?"* said Raven, disbelief clear in his voice.

"He married me because he had always liked me, and he wanted children and thought I'd be a great little mother. He thought if any woman could turn him on, it would be me. He was wrong. I couldn't have turned him on with a blowtorch! He was gay and hadn't been able to admit it!"

Janna heard the words echo in the small cabin and was appalled. She had never told anyone about that terrible night when she and her husband had both realized that he was living a lie. She wouldn't have said anything now if Raven hadn't pushed so hard. She took a long, ragged breath, wishing she could crawl under the counter to avoid Raven's dark, compassionate eyes.

"There. Feel better now?" she asked, her voice shaking.

"I was just going to ask you the same question."

"I've never felt worse in my life. Next time, leave me at the bottom of the inlet. The cost of being saved by you is too damned high."

Raven made a low, involuntary sound, as though he had been struck. "Funny," he said finally, "that's the same thing Angel told me."

Raven's lips twisted into a sad smile that tore at Janna's heart, telling her that somehow she had wounded him more deeply than she had imagined possible, far more than he had hurt her with his questions. Abruptly the anger drained out of her.

"I'm sorry," she whispered. "I didn't mean to—"

"It's all right," Raven interrupted, turning away. "You didn't know. And even if you did, I had it coming."

"If I had known, I wouldn't have said it. I'm not that cruel."

Raven turned toward Janna. "Small warrior," he said, smiling slightly as he stroked her cheek with his calloused palm. "Haven't you learned? Sometimes kindness doesn't get it done." He turned away, opened a galley drawer and pulled out a corkscrew. With a few easy, powerful motions he took the cork from the wine bottle. "Glasses are in the cupboard to your left."

Numbly Janna reached for the cupboard. She pulled two wineglasses from their restraints and faced Raven again. As he filled the glasses she could see his nostrils flare in silent appreciation of the wine's fragrance. He poured the pale golden liquid into the glasses, leaving room for the wine to be swirled by a deft movement of his wrist as he dipped his head to inhale the bouquet. The gesture spoke of a sophistication very much at odds with his rough shirt and jeans.

"What was Angel looking over her shoulder at?" Janna asked, surprising herself. She hadn't meant to ask Raven any more questions.

"A dead man."

Janna paused in the act of setting cocktail sauce on the table. "She loved him?"

"He died the night before their wedding. Her parents died in the same car crash. She survived. She was too badly injured to move. She could only lie there and listen to Grant's pain until he died."

Raven's voice was matter-of-fact, which only made the words more terrible.

Janna closed her eyes, unable to repress the shiver that took her at the thought of what Angel must have gone through. She felt ashamed of herself for lashing out at Raven. However sad and painful the end of her marriage had been, it hadn't been like watching the man she loved die and being helpless even to touch his hand.

"Angel came out of it, finally," Raven continued, putting the plate of oysters on the kitchen table.

"And you comforted her," said Janna, thinking aloud, seeing in her mind a slender blonde taking refuge from pain and grief in Raven's strong arms.

He looked sideways at Janna's pale, tight face and wondered at the sadness he saw there. "Angel had Derry—Grant's brother—to comfort her. She needed

something tougher, something that would let her pour
out all the rage she had at life for taking away the man
she loved. The rage was destroying her. She had to get
rid of it before she could cope with the despair that was
the other side of rage."

Janna's eyes opened wide as she understood. She
faced Raven and saw echoes of pain in the tight lines
bracketing his mouth. She remembered what he had
said: *Sometimes kindness doesn't get it done.* Now she
understood his words. "You deliberately made yourself
a target, didn't you?"

There was a heartbeat's pause before Raven's deep
voice said, "Yes."

"And she hated you for it."

Raven nodded.

"Didn't she ever understand why you did it?"

"She understood right away," he said, setting plates,
forks and oyster crackers on the table. "Forgiveness
took longer. Years."

"You loved her," Janna said. She was motionless,
watching Raven intently, and she was afraid in a way
that she didn't understand.

"Yes."

"You still love her."

Raven smiled gently to himself as he shifted oysters
onto Janna's plate. "Of course. Angel loves me, too,
now. You'd like her," he said, looking up. "Like you,
she's a warrior of the heart. She fought her way against
terrible odds and won life and love. A beautiful woman
in every sense of the word."

Janna looked into her wineglass and wished it were
a sea deep enough to drown in. The fear and despair she
felt were worse than they had been at the moment she
had found herself trapped beneath the sinking boat. Her

body had been cold then. Now the cold went all the way to her soul.

Fear. She was very much afraid that she had fallen in love with Raven, a man who loved someone else. Knowing the source of her fear didn't make her any less afraid. It simply made her understand her fear. She had lost something before she even had a chance to win it.

"Why aren't you married to Angel?" Janna asked flatly.

Raven gave her a swift, sideways look, then smiled. "Canada takes a dim view of bigamy."

"You're married to someone else?" Janna asked, her head snapping up, shock clear on her face.

He laughed and shook his head. "No. Angel is though, and very happily." He sipped the wine before adding quietly, "Derry and I helped Angel to survive, but it was Miles Hawkins who truly healed her. As she healed him. They brought out the best in each other. They still do."

The affection and admiration in Raven's voice when he spoke of the man Angel loved puzzled Janna. "Most men in your shoes would hate Angel's husband."

Raven's massive shoulders moved in a shrug. "Hawk gave Angel something no other man had been able to give. She gave him what she had given to no other man. They are as deeply interlocked as the sea and the shore. To hate one would be to hate the other."

Janna listened and wondered deep within herself if she would ever be able to accept the loss of love as generously as Raven had. "You're an unusual man, Carlson Raven," she said huskily. "Angel must have been blind to choose someone else."

His teeth flashed in a white smile. "You haven't met Hawk. Tall, dark, handsome, sophisticated. Wherever he goes he turns heads. Women's heads. I've never seen anything like it."

Janna looked at Raven. "Pull my other leg," she said sardonically. "It's shorter."

"Believe me, Hawk is the most—"

"He can't be a patch on you," she said succinctly, interrupting. She took a drink of her wine and then stared down into it gloomily. "My God, I'll bet there's an epidemic of female whiplash every time you walk down the street."

Raven sat at the table and cocked an inquiring black eyebrow at Janna. "Are you one of those women who can't take a sip of alcohol without getting delirious?"

With an impatient sound Janna put her wine on the table and scooped a lemon out of the sink. "Don't bother to be modest," she said, quartering the lemon with knife strokes that were just short of vicious. "Surely you've noticed the women piling up around your feet like autumn leaves."

Raven stuck his large feet out into the aisle and looked at them curiously. "Nope. Not a one."

"Of course not," she shot back. "You have two."

"More than six and a half, actually."

Janna blinked. "Help."

"Feet," he added blandly. "As in tall."

Smiling, shaking her head, Janna gave up. The last of her anger fled as she looked at Raven's dark face animated by inner laughter. For a tearing instant she wondered why life was so unfair as to give Raven everything she had ever wanted in a man—and then to place him beyond her reach. Sudden tears came in blinding counterpoint to laughter, threatening to choke her. She tried to speak, to explain, but all that came out were fragments of Raven's name.

"Hey, it wasn't that bad a pun," Raven said gently, coming to stand beside Janna and blot up her tears with a napkin.

Head down, leaning against his strength, Janna fought not to cry. After a minute she succeeded.

"Sorry," she said, drawing a deep breath. "I never cry. I don't know what's wrong." She sighed and reluctantly drew back from Raven's body.

"You had quite a scare a few days ago," Raven said quietly. His hand hesitated before he permitted himself the luxury of stroking Janna's gleaming cinnamon hair. The smooth warmth of the crown of her head made his palm feel as though it was caressing fire. "It's not surprising you're still feeling the emotional aftershocks."

Janna felt Raven's touch all the way to the soles of her feet. She wanted to turn her head and catch his hard palm against her lips. Even as the impulse came, she had given in to it. Her lips brushed over his warm hand.

"You're very kind," she said huskily. "Whoever Hawk is, whatever he is, Angel took second best."

Raven watched as Janna turned from his arms and slid into the booth seat along the table. Her honesty and vulnerability to him made him ache with tenderness. And hunger. He knew that she wanted him. He knew how much he wanted her. Silently he cursed the circumstances that had brought them together and at the same time made it impossible for him to accept what she offered. He couldn't take a woman who came to him out of a combination of misplaced gratitude and primitive survival instincts.

And that was all Janna was feeling now—gratitude and the emotional aftershocks of almost dying. She would have been equally drawn to any man who had saved her life and then cared for her.

Too bad he wouldn't have been equally drawn to any woman he had fished out of the sea.

Grimly Raven's big hand closed around his wineglass. He took a quick swallow, then another, as though the beautiful Chardonnay were medicine. And, in a way, it was. If he drank enough of it he might sleep tonight instead of lying awake so frustrated and aroused that he could count his own pulse in the rigid stirrings of his sex.

With an abrupt movement Raven sat down, concealing his physical turmoil beneath the opaque barrier of the table. A hard smile tugged at his mouth as he eyed the oysters heaped on his plate. If folk tales were true, right now he needed saltpeter a hell of a lot more than he needed oysters.

Janna reached for the oyster crackers, shook out a handful and offered Raven the package. He took it without a word. She wondered what he was thinking that had etched such an odd smile onto his lips. When she realized that she was watching those same chiseled lips with breathless intensity, she looked away, flushing guiltily.

"What do you do when you aren't fishing tourists out of Totem Inlet?" Janna asked, seizing the first words that came into her mind.

"I used to be a commercial fisherman." Raven squeezed lemon onto an oyster and forked it into his mouth. "Not bad," he said thoughtfully, appreciating the acid tang of fresh lemon.

"The oyster?" she asked, pausing in the act of reaching for one of her own.

"The lemon."

Janna blinked. "Don't you usually have it with oysters?"

"No."

"Then why did you have all those lemons on board?"

"Angel likes fresh lemonade. We were going to

cruise the east side of Moresby Island for a few days until Hawk got back from Tokyo. Hawk got in early, though." Raven smiled crookedly. "Married nearly four years and he still hates being away from Angel."

"Maybe he didn't want to tempt fate by leaving Angel alone with you," Janna said dryly.

Raven smiled even as he shook his head. "Not a chance. Pass some of that sauce over this way," he said. "I'll try it next."

"Haven't you ever had this kind of sauce on your oysters?" she asked, nudging the dish full of cocktail sauce closer to him.

"Nope," Raven rumbled.

"Then why did you have ketchup and horseradish on board?"

"For my roast beef sandwiches." He dipped an oyster in the dish, chewed the succulent flesh and cocked his head thoughtfully. "Not bad. Kind of saucy."

Janna winced at the awful pun. "How do you usually eat your oysters? Cooked in a stew?"

"Just the way I find them. In the raw."

"Must be kind of chilly," she said, reaching for her third oyster.

"What?"

"Finding oysters in the raw. Most people wear shirts and jeans and…"

Janna ducked a casual swipe from Raven's massive hand. When she straightened again, his fingers returned to tuck a stray lock of hair behind her ear.

"We're going to have to find you a scarf the color of your eyes."

The gentleness of Raven's touch made Janna's heart stop and then beat with redoubled speed even as she told herself it was just a casual gesture that meant nothing.

And even though it had made her go all shivery, it certainly hadn't affected him. He was picking up his glass of wine as though nothing had happened.

Raven drained his glass in a single motion, cursing himself for touching Janna at every excuse—and knowing that he was just waiting for another tendril of silky hair to escape so that he could touch her again. He looked at his wineglass. Empty. Janna's was almost empty, too. He refilled both glasses and wished that he and Janna were as naked as the oysters gleaming within their pearly half shells.

"To oysters in the raw," Raven said, lifting his wineglass.

His slow, very male smile sent frissons of awareness through Janna. She touched her wineglass to his and drank quickly, deeply, grateful for the excuse to look away from Raven's midnight eyes. If he smiled like that again, she was afraid she would crawl right into his lap and beg to be kissed.

The thought shocked her. She took another quick swallow of wine and felt a different kind of warmth spread through her. Belatedly she realized that wine probably wasn't what she should be drinking; alcohol wasn't noted for enhancing self-control. On the other hand, the wine was absolutely delicious. Probably far too delicious.

"Do you still fish commercially?" Janna asked, firmly trading wineglass for oyster fork.

"I own several commercial boats," Raven said. "My cousins have fished them for the last three years while I took Hawk's money and saw the world."

"Hawk must be as generous as he is handsome."

Raven smiled crookedly. "Technically the money's mine, but Hawk is the one who made it for me. The man's a bloody genius with investments and land. Not long after he and Angel met, I gave him a few thousand dollars. A year later he gave me back a few million."

Gray-green eyes wide with shock, Janna reached for her wineglass again, despite the vague light-headedness that was stealing through her. The idea that Raven was wealthy unnerved her, placing him even farther beyond her reach. She drank a healthy swallow of wine and told herself that she was a fool. She needed more wits about her, not less.

On the other hand, wine's anesthetic properties had never seemed more appealing. She drank again.

"I lost most of it the following year," Raven said matter-of-factly. "Storms and fickle fish. Hawk just laughed and showed me how to make it all over again."

Janna waved her wineglass in a vague circle that took in the *Black Star*. "Looks like you're doing a good job of it."

Raven shrugged and dipped another oyster in the thick sauce. "Like Hawk says, money's just a way of keeping score. It's nothing to build a life around. Angel is, though, and he knows it. Smart man, Hawk." Raven chewed the oyster thoughtfully. "Still a bit saucy."

"Is that what you're doing?"

"Being saucy?" he asked innocently.

But Janna didn't smile. Questions were crowding her tongue, reckless questions fueled by frustration and potent wine. "Are you building your life around Angel, too?" she asked, forking up another oyster.

The smile vanished from Raven's face, leaving behind the silence and blunt strength that was his very core. "I'm not a fool, Janna," he said quietly. "Angel will never love anyone but Hawk. He feels the same way about her."

"And so do you," Janna said bleakly.

She drank more wine, hoping that it would finish the job of numbing her brain that the first glass had already begun. Her tongue, however, wasn't yet numb. She had drunk just enough wine to say whatever came to her and let the chips hit the fan. Vaguely she realized that wasn't quite what chips were supposed to do. Well, the chips would just have to look out for themselves. She lifted her glass in a mocking toast.

"To love," she said. "The best antidote to happiness yet devised by man."

The bitterness in Janna's voice surprised Raven. His eyes narrowed as he saw the unhappiness the wine had revealed beneath Janna's humor.

"You aren't drinking," she noted.

Raven said nothing.

"Ah well," said Janna carelessly, shrugging, "not everyone likes the truth. There are times when I sure as hell don't." She drained her glass.

"And what is the truth?" he asked in a deep voice.

"You're hung up on Angel."

"There have been other women in my life."

"But only one Angel," Janna retorted recklessly. "The perfect willowy blond, green eyes full of mysteries and tragedy. Meanwhile the rest of the women in the world can forget it. Whatever they have to offer you isn't wanted."

"That's not true."

Janna muttered something succinct and contradictory beneath her breath as she reached for the wine bottle. It was empty. Startled, she looked at Raven's glass. It was also empty.

"More wine?" he asked smoothly. "This is getting interesting. *In vino veritas* to coin an old phrase."

"I have just enough brains left to know that more

wine would be a really dumb idea for me," Janna said, stabbing an oyster so hard that her fork grated on the shell. "But don't let that stop you. I've been on a roll lately. One dumb thing after another. Next thing you know I'll be bleaching my hair and learning the harp and shopping for paper wings. Sure, bring on the wine. Fantastic idea. Should have thought of it sooner. Does wine make you tragic and mysterious, too?"

"What in hell are you talking about?" Raven asked in a mild tone.

"Wining and dining," Janna said, waving an oyster at him.

"Was that with or without an *h*?" he asked blandly, but his eyes gleamed with suppressed laughter.

For an instant Janna didn't understand. Then she heard the echoes of her own bitter words coming back to her. "Whining," she whispered too softly for Raven to hear.

"Of course," he continued, "most oysters do tend to complain when dining with a walrus. From their point of view…" He saw the brittle animation suddenly leave Janna's face, revealing the pain beneath. He curled his hand comfortingly over hers. "Janna? I was joking."

"Yes, of course," she said automatically. She looked at the big hand covering her own and knew that she couldn't keep up the pretense any longer. Her hand slid from beneath his.

"Excuse me," she said carefully. "I've had about all the comfort I can handle for one night. I have some sketching I should do while the images are still fresh in my mind."

Without waiting for Raven's answer, Janna grabbed the tablet and pencil from the counter. She retreated to her bunk in the bow, shutting the small door behind her, leaving her words to echo in Raven's mind.

*I've had about all the comfort I can handle for one night.*

Raven didn't know that his hand had clenched into a fist until he heard the sudden shattering of the wine-glass. Slowly he opened his hand and let the glittering fragments fall to the table. Absently he wiped the bright dust from his palm. He should have known better than to buy such fragile glasses. He wasn't any good with fragile things. Too damned big. Too damned strong. Too damned brutal. The really fine things of life were invariably crushed within his grasp. Like Angel.

And like Janna.

Raven leaned his head back against the bulkhead, closed his eyes and swore tiredly.

## Chapter 6

Raven awakened instantly, silently, completely. His senses told him that the storm was over. The wind was little more than a fading whisper. The *Black Star* lay almost motionless beneath him. Moonlight poured in silver torrents through openings in the spent clouds.

And nearby, someone was crying very softly.

Before Raven could stop himself, he was halfway out of bed and heading for Janna's bunk in the bow. With an effort of will he forced himself to lie down again. If he went to her, he would give her more than comfort. He would lie beside her and caress her until those beautiful legs opened for him. Then he would slide his hard, violently sensitive flesh into her softness, finding the sweet and wild union that he had been aching for ever since he had seen her struggling so bravely against the storm.

Even as Raven tried to tell himself that surely he could comfort Janna without making love to her, he knew that it wasn't true. His whole body was flushed with sexual heat, pulsing with the hard beating of his heart. He had never felt so close to the limit of his self-control with a woman. The need to comfort and ravish, to soothe and incite, to find wildness and peace within Janna was tearing him apart.

Grimly Raven lay very still, fighting his unruly body and his equally unruly emotions, knowing that it would be a long time before he got to sleep again. He had been a long time getting to sleep in the first place. He had waited for hours for Janna to stop sketching and come out of the bow cabin so that he could apologize to her in the relative safety of the main cabin. Finally he had been able to stand it no longer. He had knocked at the tiny door to her cabin. There had been a long hesitation before she had answered. Her tone had been subdued, almost flat. He had realized then how much life she usually had in her voice. The difference had gone into him like a knife.

Remembering the lack of music in Janna's voice did nothing to ease the restlessness in Raven's body right now. Nor did hearing the muffled, ragged sounds of her fighting not to cry out loud help him to be at peace. Finally, after what seemed far too long, the soft noises faded, merging with the subtle whisper of the wind. Raven sighed in relief and went back to counting silver salmon on the back of his eyelids.

The sound of the bow door furtively opening brought every nerve in Raven's massive body alive. He heard Janna tiptoe up the two steps into the main cabin. He sensed her crowding against the far side of the aisle that separated his bunk from the galley stove. His nostrils flared as her subtle, indefinable fragrance washed over him like moonlight while she eased past his bunk to the door leading to the stern.

Hands clenched into fists to keep from reaching out to her, Raven listened as Janna passed his bunk in an almost soundless rush of hurrying feet. The cabin door opened, letting in a gust of cool midnight air. Janna stood briefly in the luminous moonlight before she slipped through the door. Raven closed his eyes. It didn't help. He could still see the firm, moon-silvered rise of her breasts beneath one of his old T-shirts. He wondered if she was wearing the dark lace panties beneath or if nothing except night concealed her vulnerable softness.

It seemed an unreasonably long time before Janna stealthily opened and closed the stern door again and began easing past Raven's bunk on her way back down the narrow aisle to the bow cabin. He listened to the soft sounds of her approach, smelled the mixed fragrance of womanly warmth and the coolness of rain-washed night. He was congratulating himself on keeping his hands to himself when he saw the gleam of tears on her cheeks.

"Janna," he whispered, reaching out and wrapping his hand around her wrist with a reflexive hunger that he had denied too long. "Janna, what's wrong? No, don't pull back. I won't hurt you. I just want to comfort you."

And it was true, as far as it went. He did want to comfort her. He wanted it as much as he wanted her.

Janna trembled when she felt the power of Raven's hand wrapped warmly around her wrist.

"Janna?" he said softly. "Talk to me."

"I just needed some air," she said, trying to control her ragged breathing. She felt like a prize fool. She hadn't cried in years, yet since she had met Raven, she rained as regularly as the clouds.

"You're crying."

"Think of it—" Her voice broke. She took a breath and finished in a rush, "Think of it as Queen Charlotte s-sunshine."

Raven's hand tightened almost painfully on Janna's arm, then eased to a caress as he ran his fingertips slowly over the softness of her inner wrist. Janna's breath came in with a raggedness that had nothing to do with tears.

"I'm sorry," he said, his voice so deep that it was as much felt as heard. "I didn't mean to hurt you with that crack about whining and dining. I thought you would—"

"That's all right," she interrupted hurriedly. Her words were quick, staccato, like cold rain whipped by a storm wind. "I was whining. There's no need for you to—to apologize for telling the truth."

"Damn it, that's not what I meant!" Raven snarled.

"I understand. Really." Janna felt her control dissolving again and wanted to crawl off somewhere before she humiliated herself even further. "Raven," she said brokenly, "please let go." Vainly she tried to pull her wrist free of his warm, immovable grip. "I'm sorry I woke you. I'm s-sorry I—oh, God, please let go of me!"

There was an instant of silence before Raven's powerful arm flexed and he pulled Janna onto the bunk, into his arms. He had just enough self-control not to kick back the covers and hold her along his hungry, naked length.

"It's all right," Raven said, stroking Janna's hair and her back, ignoring her struggles to free herself. "Go ahead, small warrior," he murmured. "Cry while I hold you. Hold me if you want to. Please, Janna. I would never have said anything about whining if I had thought you would take me seriously. You've been so brave, so full of laughter. I expected you to sling an oyster at me with a smart remark about the dangers of going for a walk with a walrus, but instead you believed what was meant to be a silly joke. Can you forgive me?"

Janna made a strangled sound that could have come from tears or laughter or an aching combination of both.

Raven's arms closed around her, rocking her gently against his huge chest. When her own arms finally stirred and crept around his neck, he felt both relief and a hunger whose violent intensity shocked him, telling him that he was even closer to the edge of his control than he had realized. His only consolation was that Janna was lying across his chest. As long as she didn't change position, she wouldn't know what she was doing to him.

*So tell her. Better yet, show her,* Raven advised himself sardonically. *She's much too generous and vulnerable to turn me away. She thinks she wants me. She's so damned grateful to me that she'd do anything I asked. She'd do everything. And it would be so hot, so good.*

The fugitive thoughts glittered within the darkness of Raven's mind, darting and gleaming like salmon trying to evade the net. All that kept him from giving in to his hunger was the knowledge that he would hate himself for taking advantage of Janna's vulnerability.

"What was that about an oyster and a walrus?" Janna asked finally, sighing and relaxing utterly against Raven's chest.

He smiled and brushed his lips so lightly over Janna's hair that she didn't feel the touch. "Didn't your brothers ever explain what happens when a tender, innocent, succulent little oyster goes out wining and dining with a walrus?" he asked.

Janna shook her head, afraid to trust her voice.

"Your education has been dangerously neglected."

Raven's deep voice vibrated through her, pervading her to her core, melting her with laughter and heat. Unconsciously she moved her cheek across his chest, snuggling even closer to his warmth. His arms tightened fractionally, shifting the softness of her breasts against him. Heat surged through him like chain lightning, setting fires in his male flesh.

"'Twas brillig and the slithy toves/Did gyre and gimble in the wabe…'" Raven quoted deeply, ignoring the hot, hard stirring of his aroused body.

This time he was sure that laughter was causing the soft sounds and softer movements that Janna made against him. He took in a long breath and told himself all the reasons why he would be an insensitive, unforgivable, contemptible, rotten son of a bitch if he took advantage of her now.

Janna lifted her head, looked Raven in the eye and said, "Frumious bandersnatch."

"Gesundheit," he said instantly.

Her lips quivered with the effort of holding back her laughter, but she gamely stuck with it. "It was the frumious bandersnatch that gyred and gimbled in the wabe," she explained. "Not a walrus. If you don't believe me, ask Lewis Carroll."

"Carroll was too busy waxing his ceilings and shoeing cabbages for kings to worry about who was or wasn't gyre-ing and gimble-ing in or out of wabes," Raven retorted.

Laughter and sudden tears trembled on the brink of release as Janna looked at Raven loving him, wanting him. She sighed his name and brushed her lips over his. He returned the soft kiss until the tip of her tongue traced his upper lip. Then he turned away and very gently tucked Janna's head against his shoulder.

It was the most exquisitely tender rejection that Janna could imagine; and it wounded her as no other ever could, sliding through her defenses like a silver razor, slicing her open all the way to her soul, leaving her helpless to do anything but curl up inside with pain.

Raven felt the difference in her instantly, a stillness and a withdrawal so complete that he couldn't believe he was still holding her. "Janna?"

After a long moment she straightened and eased free of Raven's arms until she could stand in the narrow aisle between his bunk and the galley. She looked down at his powerful body swathed in the dark sheet, at moonlight caught in the transparent black clarity of his eyes, at the big hand held out to her. Even now she could feel the imprint of his warmth on her skin, taste him on the tip of her tongue. She wanted him so much that it was like dying to know that he didn't want her at all.

"What's wrong?" he asked.

"Nothing new," Janna said finally, unconsciously echoing Raven's earlier words to her. She felt the heat and chills of humiliation slowly ebbing, leaving behind only pain and a determination not to make things more uncomfortable for the man who had been so terribly kind and patient with her. "I'm sorry about the kiss, Raven," she whispered. "Truly I am. I keep thinking that I have something to give a man in bed. I'm a slow learner. Really slow. Sorry."

"Janna—damn it! There's nothing wrong with you!" Raven said harshly, feeling his control evaporating. He had wanted to spare her, not to hurt her more. Yet everything he said or did only made it worse. Somehow he had to make her understand that it wasn't that she didn't turn him on; it was that she wanted him for all the wrong reasons. "It's the situation, not you. If we'd met any other way than—"

"Don't," she said, cutting across his words. Then, very gently, she said again, "Don't, Raven. You don't have to lie to me. I'm a big girl. I can stand the truth. And the truth is that I lack whatever that indefinable something is that arouses a man. I'm sorry I embarrassed you. I promise that it won't happen again." Janna forced a smile and held out her right hand. "Friends?"

"Friends?" gritted Raven. He stared up at Janna, his eyes as black as night itself. Her smile was infuriating, as brilliant and empty as the moonlight pouring over her outstretched hand. *"Friends?"* he repeated, smiling savagely as he reached for her.

There was no warning. One instant Janna was standing in the aisle with a social smile plastered on her face and the next instant she was flat on her back in Raven's bed with his powerful, naked leg across her thighs, pinning her to the mattress.

"Oh yes," he said thickly, "we're friends, Janna." He took both her hands, and as he spoke he began dragging them down the length of his body. "I'm a great believer in friends being honest with each other."

"Raven? What…?"

The question ended in a gasp as Janna felt Raven's unmistakable male hardness beneath her hands.

"That's what," he rasped.

Raven was so aroused that she could feel the heavy beat of his pulse as he closed her fingers around him. He felt hot and tight to the point of bursting.

"It's been like that damn near all the time since I saw

you fighting the storm," he said flatly. "You smile or you turn around or you lick your lips, and I get so hot all I can think about is opening your legs and burying myself in you. If you give me any more crap about not being sexy enough to turn a man on I'm going to…"

The words became a broken groan as Janna's fingers moved over Raven slowly, savoring every bit of his erect male flesh. His hips moved reflexively, stroking his hungry length between her caressing hands. He saw her looking at his body, smiling at the very visible proof of his desire for her. He shuddered heavily, moving against her warm hands, feeling a pleasure so intense that he clenched his teeth against a guttural cry.

"No more," Raven said finally, his voice ragged. He caught Janna's face between his big hands. "I won't take you. It wouldn't be fair to you. I just wanted you to know that I've never had a woman turn me on so hard, so quick. If you were any sexier to me, I'd come just looking at you. How's that for honest?"

Janna looked up at Raven's face. His eyes were narrowed, glittering, and his mouth was drawn back as though in pain. His skin was hot to her touch, gleaming with sweat, and every powerful muscle was rigid with passion and control. He stirred hungrily between her hands with each rapid heartbeat, a man more potent than she had ever dreamed. The knowledge that he wanted her so much was a searing wildness racing through her, melting her with a sensual heat that she had never before known. She shivered repeatedly, hotly, tiny convulsions that changed her body within the space of a few breaths. She tried to speak but could not, she could only moan his name as her own buried sensuality burst within her, drenching her with liquid fire.

The scent of her arousal made Raven's whole body

tighten. As though in a hot dream he felt her passionate shivering while her legs shifted, opening for him, pleading for him as her hands drew him closer to her.

"Janna—no." And then Raven groaned, feeling the softness and moisture of her. "Oh God," he said through clenched teeth as she melted at the first touch of him, bathing him with her heat. "I can't do this to you. I haven't even kissed you. You deserve better than this."

"We're kissing now," Janna whispered.

She moved her hips until Raven's hot flesh nuzzled against her softness, letting him feel what the honesty of his desire had done to her. He wanted to tell Janna to stop before it was too late, but he couldn't speak. What she was doing took his breath away. His hands clenched on the T-shirt she wore as he fought not to lose control.

And then it was too late. The shirt ripped from neck to hem as he took her with a single powerful thrust of his hips, burying himself in her. She was sleek and ready and wonderfully tight. He had never felt anything half so good. He withdrew and drove into her again and then again, measuring her taut, welcoming softness with his own hard flesh. He knew he should slow down but it was too late for that, it had been too late since he had first seen her fighting the storm. He had never lost control with a woman but it was happening now, everything spinning away from him as pleasure burst repeatedly, wildly, shaking him to his soul. With a hoarse sound that was Janna's name, he poured himself into her, knowing only her and the sweet violence of the release she had given to him.

Janna felt the wild trembling of Raven's body, heard her name a ragged cry on his lips and held him fiercely, savoring every instant of his shuddering climax. The knowledge that he had wanted her so badly and that he had found such a complete release within her moved her in ways that she couldn't describe. Tears spilled down her cheeks as she held Raven, loving the feel of him in her arms and in her body, feeling love for him like a fierce, sweet agony in her soul, wanting nothing more from life but to hold him until she died.

Finally Raven's breathing settled into the slow rhythms of relaxation and he stirred as though to roll aside. Janna's arms tightened in silent protest. She didn't want it to end. Not yet. Not ever. His thick mustache brushed over her cheek in a silky caress as he kissed her gently and then kissed her again, nibbling softly until his lips met the warm trail of her tears. He stiffened and drew back until he could see the shining evidence against her cheek.

"My God," he said, his voice breaking. "I'm sorry, Janna. I didn't mean to hurt you."

"No," she said quickly, holding Raven as he tried to withdraw from her. "You didn't hurt me."

But even as she spoke, he gently eased from her body, his strength making a mockery of her attempts to hold him. As he left her she cried out softly. He stroked her hair with a hand that trembled.

"I'm sorry," he whispered, "so sorry. I've never lost control like that. I just wanted you too much. I forgot how strong I am, how I'm no good with fragile things. I'm sorry, Janna. God, I—" His voice broke again.

Raven closed his eyes and fought for the control that seemed to elude him every time he was close to Janna. She heard the raw emotion in his voice and saw the wild glitter of unshed tears in his eyes. With wondering fingertips she caressed his cheek and the thick black curve of his closed eyelashes.

"You didn't hurt me," she said huskily.

"You're crying," he said in a harsh tone. "I must have hurt like hell."

"No," she said, putting her fingers across his warm lips. "Listen to me, Raven. You didn't hurt. It was knowing how much you wanted me, having you inside me, feeling you fill me with your hunger and need." The words stopped in a ragged breath. "It was unbearably beautiful," she whispered, kissing him. "That's why I cried. That's why I'm still crying."

Raven's hand moved against a bulkhead switch. Instantly a soft golden light flooded the bunk. As though to reassure himself of the truth of her words, he went swiftly over her body with his fingertips, searching for any sign that he had hurt her in the violence of his own need.

With wide eyes Janna watched Raven, trembling as he gently parted her legs and touched her with exquisite care. Heat bloomed unexpectedly, making her breath catch. He heard the tiny sound and touched her again, wondering if he had hurt her despite her assurances that he had not. Very lightly he traced the incredible softness of her, expecting her to flinch. She made another stifled sound as he circled her again, seeking her most tender flesh. She shivered helplessly as she melted at his touch.

Raven's expression changed, became both gentle and…hungry. He caressed Janna again, melting her again, smiling as he felt the proof that he hadn't hurt her. When his hand pressed against her leg, she shifted unconsciously, giving herself to his touch, watching him while his dark glance moved over her in another kind of caress. She looked down at herself and realized that she was wearing his torn T-shirt like an open vest. The thin cotton clung to her breasts, held by the dampness of her flushed body, and his big hand was curved protectively, possessively, around the vulnerable softness that she had given to him.

"Small warrior," Raven whispered as his hand rubbed slowly against Janna. "So soft, so hot, so generous."

Eyes wide and luminous, Janna lay on the rumpled sheets, watching Raven while he caressed her, feeling as though he were stroking her with silk and fire. Slowly, very slowly, his fingertips smoothed up her body, leaving heat and dampness in their wake. The sensual contrast with the cool air of the cabin made her tremble.

Then Raven's long index finger finally slid beneath the torn cotton T-shirt, tracing and freeing a breast in the same motion. Janna's nipple tightened in a tingling rush. She watched his fingertip stroke slowly across her ribs, sliding closer to her other breast. Before he even touched it, the hard rise of her nipple was clear beneath the cotton. Raven's smile as he peeled aside the clinging cloth made her breath wedge in her throat.

"Raven?" she whispered.

He made a rumbling sound that could have meant anything as he traced her tight, velvety peak. She watched in helpless fascination when he bent and touched the dark nipple with the tip of his tongue. A ragged sound came from her that could have been his name. His answer was a husky male laugh and the tender pressure of his teeth closing over her nipple, tugging at her, unraveling her breath and her body in a few rushing instants. She called his name in what she meant to be a question but came out as a broken cry.

"Yes," Raven said, understanding the question Janna hadn't been able to ask. He nuzzled her breast and the curve of her throat, tasting her with obvious pleasure. "I'm going to eat every sweet bit of you. But first I'm going to find out if your mouth is as hot and wild and welcoming as your body is." He laughed again, a sound so low that it was more felt than heard. "I've never learned a woman's secrets in reverse order before," he murmured, holding himself back long enough to admire Janna's mouth. "Once I had learned the last secret, the others didn't interest me. But you do, small warrior. I ache to know if you'll open these lips as trustingly as you opened the rest of yourself."

Janna saw the sensual curves of Raven's mouth and the black, silky gleam of his mustache as he slowly lowered his head. She tried to say his name but could not. Her lips parted for him on a husky sigh. She felt the tiny shudder that took him as he brought his mouth to hers, joining them as completely as he had joined their bodies a few minutes ago.

When Janna felt the hot touch of his tongue, her whole body tightened with a surge of pleasure. His taste swept through her, filling her senses. The tip of his tongue found hers and teased it as he had once teased her breast. She made an inarticulate sound and ran her fingers across the powerful muscles of his shoulders, testing his resilience. As he felt the tiny bite of her nails his tongue thrust deeply into her and withdrew almost instantly, as though he were afraid of hurting her.

"Again," Janna whispered, burying her fingers in the thickness of Raven's hair, pulling his head down to her. "Oh, please, kiss me like that again."

He took her words and her mouth with a hoarse sound, kissing her so fiercely that her neck arched across the muscular thickness of his forearm. With an effort he brought himself under control again.

"You're pure hell on my good intentions," Raven said huskily, looking at Janna's reddened lips with a combination of regret and raw hunger.

She looked up at his narrowed eyes and licked her lips uncertainly. They tingled and felt hot and sensitive, and she wanted nothing more than to feel herself crushed within Raven's arms again.

"What do you mean?" Janna whispered, touching her tongue to her lips again.

He smiled. "Lick my lips like that and I'll show you."

Janna's eyes widened. Her hands slid up to his cheeks and she held him as she pulled herself toward his mouth. She licked his lips slowly, loving the feel of his breath rushing hotly over her as he groaned. His fingers thrust deeply into her hair, pulling her head back until her neck was a creamy offering to his mouth and he could see her pulse beat heavily beneath her skin. He bit her lips with sensual restraint even as he held her arched helplessly between his powerful hands.

Shivering, watching his eyes, she breathed his name.

"What do you like from a man?" Raven asked. "Tell me and it's yours. Whatever you want, however you want it, for as long as you can take it. Just tell me."

"I don't know," she admitted. "My husband never wanted this." Janna's breath caught, then came out with a ragged sound as Raven's teeth closed delicately over the pulse beating in her throat.

"You told me all I need to know about your husband," Raven said, nuzzling against the sensitive lobe of her ear. "Now tell me what you wanted from your lovers."

"I don't know. You're the only one I ever had."

Janna felt Raven become utterly still. Slowly his

head came up until he could look into her eyes. She tried to make a joke of her inexperience but the words stuck in her throat.

"Ever?" he asked, hardly able to believe that a woman as sensual and generous as Janna had never found a man to enjoy her.

"I didn't think anyone would want me. Not really. I even read a whole shelf of how-to manuals for Mark but it didn't help."

Her words ended in a soft, tearing sound as Raven's tongue thrust into her ear. She moaned softly, and her nails bit into the flexed muscles of his chest.

"Books, huh?" growled Raven, biting her ear sensually, teasing her with his tongue, feeling heat burst through him at her helpless response. He laughed softly and thrust his tongue into her ear as his teeth gently devoured her. "Let me know if I miss any paragraphs that intrigued you."

"What?" Janna asked, not understanding anything except the sensations marching over her skin, heat and cold and pleasure impossibly mingling until she shivered.

"I'm going to love you, Janna. All of you," Raven said in a deep voice, biting her neck with enough force to leave small marks. "I'm going to love you until you moan and cry and come apart. And then I'm going to start all over again, and then again, until you would kill or die to have me inside you. That's when I'll take you and you'll take me, all of me, and it will be so good you'll scream."

It was a sensuous threat and a sensual promise, and Janna wanted both to come true. As she reached for Raven, his fingers laced through hers and he pulled her hands above her head. His black, glittering eyes and elemental male smile made her whole body arch as she tried to reach him, wanting to know the hot penetration of his body once again. When he saw the helpless movement of her legs he smiled and then swore lightly when his body went hard in a single wild rush. He shouldn't want her again this soon, this much, as though he had never taken her at all. But he did.

And if he let himself look at her hungry softness any longer, he would take her.

Janna gasped as she felt herself picked up and turned onto her stomach as though she weighed nothing. She started to ask a question, then forgot what she had wanted to say as his hands slid beneath her, capturing her breasts. Heat shivered through her as he kneaded her sensitive flesh until her nipples were hard and her breathing was ragged. She sensed his breath on her spine in the instant before his teeth closed on her nape. Caught between his caressing hands and his mouth, Janna moaned his name softly.

"Raven, I want to hold you," she said.

She made a broken sound as strong fingers rolled her nipples caressingly, tightening them until fire burst deep in the pit of her stomach. Her leg flexed in helpless response as she tried to roll onto her side, instinctively seeking the fulfillment of his body within hers. His knee slid between her legs, pinning her, making it impossible for her to roll over.

"Don't you want me to hold you?" she said.

"Oh, I want it," he said through clenched teeth. "Too much. You're so damned sexy you make me lose control," he gritted. "Can't you feel what you do to me?"

Janna felt the rigid power of Raven against her hip. She moved slowly, caressing and enjoying him in the

only way that she could. A husky groan was her reward.
Then his hand moved, raking tenderly down her spine
until his fingers found the warm crease between her
hips. He followed that down and down until he could
hold her in his palm once more.

"All that heat waiting," Raven whispered as his teeth
sank sensually into Janna's hip. He laughed deep in his
throat as he stroked her with his hard palm, hardly able
to believe that she wanted him so much. He said her
name against her skin again and again, leaving sensual
marks each time.

Janna barely heard. Raven's caressing palm was
stripping away her breath, her thoughts, her control. Instinctively she shifted, making more room for him
between her legs, wanting more of the incredibly
sensual touch. Callused fingertips moved slowly,
seeking out and caressing her most sensitive flesh until
she made a broken sound and her hips moved with his
touch. He rewarded her with another love bite that made
her moan. He felt her warmth seep over him at the
gently stinging caress and heard her cry of pleasure.

"God," he said hoarsely, turning Janna over so that
he could bite the soft heat of her inner thigh. "You make
me want to cover you everywhere with loving marks."
He turned and nuzzled the hot secrets that awaited him.
"Everywhere," he said huskily as his teeth closed on her
with exquisite care.

Sensations raced through Janna, making her
tremble violently.

"Raven, I—"

"You taste like the sea," he said. "Salty, mysterious, wild."

When Raven parted Janna's legs with his hands, she
gave him what he asked without hesitation, abandon-

ing herself to him because there was no other choice. The tight nub of her passion was no longer hidden from him. He had found it and his sweet, hungry caresses were making her helpless. Her back arched as something wild speared through her, tightening her whole body.

"Raven?" she cried, sinking her nails heedlessly into his shoulders because he was the only thing real in a world that was coming apart in slow motion around her. "Raven!"

His only answer was a low sound as his teeth closed around her with dark restraint, holding her captive for his loving. His name broke from her lips in fragments as tension coiled within her body more tightly with each instant. She called his name again, frightened now, wholly at the mercy of the sensations spearing through her with every hot caress.

"It's all right," he said huskily, "I won't hurt you." He kissed her very gently, cherishing her tender flesh. "Give yourself to me, small warrior. Let me love you."

"Yes," she whispered as he kissed her again. "Oh, yes."

And then the heat and hunger of Raven's loving stripped the world away, leaving ecstasy in its place. His hands gripped Janna's hips, holding her against him as he caressed her, increasing the wild pleasure sleeting through her, listening to the husky cries he had called from her.

When the last shivering finally faded from Janna, Raven moved slowly up her body, licking the mist of passion from her skin. He wanted her with a violence that shook him, but he made no move to take her. He knew that she had found her release; he didn't expect her to want him now.

"Raven," she said, blindly seeking his lips. "Hold me. Please, hold me."

He felt her tears against his cheek and wrapped his arms tightly around her, finding both relief and torment in pressing his erect flesh against her.

"Be inside me," she whispered, touching him with loving fingers. The thought of being joined with him again made her tremble. "Let me hold all of you, Raven. Let me feel you moving inside me. Please."

Raven closed his eyes and struggled for control. He knew that Janna might as well have been a virgin, that he shouldn't take her again so soon. And he knew that if he didn't feel himself sheathed within her loving softness again he would die.

"Janna—" he began, trying to explain why it would be better for her if they waited.

"You were right," Janna interrupted, whispering against Raven's mouth as her nails bit into his powerful back, urging him closer to her. "I would kill or die to have you inside me."

Emotion swept through Raven, changing everything as the world shifted and faded away, leaving only the woman who watched him with luminous silver-green eyes. "I'll hurt you," he said harshly.

"No," Janna said, moving her hips so that Raven pressed gently against her softness. "I was made for your loving."

Raven felt the spreading heat of Janna's pleasure and wanted her even more now than he had the first time.

"Are you sure?" he asked huskily, easing into her even as he asked, ready to withdraw at the least sign of her discomfort.

"Oh, yes, I'm sure," she said throatily, feeling the

secret, hot movements of her body as pleasure shimmered deep within her again.

Raven felt Janna's pleasure as clearly as she did. He made a thick sound and took her mouth, kissing her deeply, moving slowly within her, drinking her soft cries of love. She was heat and a glittering promise surrounding him, calling to him, loving him. She sank into him like the mist into the forest, inseparable, penetrating his very core, filling him even as he filled her; and then ecstasy swept through them in a wild silver wind, stirring them until they cried out and clung to each other, knowing only each other, letting everything else spin away into darkness.

## Chapter 7

Janna awoke slowly, dreaming that she was lying out in the sun with heat pouring over her in a golden cascade. She smiled and stirred slowly, arching herself into the warmth.

Raven smoothed his hand down Janna's body again, enjoying her uninhibited sensuality. When he had discovered that she had never taken a lover, he had felt both fiercely proud—and guilty. He believed that if he hadn't saved her life, if they hadn't been locked up together in the inlet's savage, beautiful Eden, Janna wouldn't have wanted him any more than she had wanted other men.

Yet he had taken advantage of their isolation and her gratitude anyway, because he had never wanted a woman so much.

It was the same right now. He wanted Janna. Right or wrong, passion or gratitude, Eden or hell. He wanted her. She was the sound of laughter on the wind and a wild silver mist glittering within his soul. She was the mysterious taste of the sea and the hot generosity of life itself. He would have given the blood from his veins to believe that she would have come to him no matter where and how they had met.

But he knew that it wasn't true. If they had met in a normal way, she would have taken one look at his intimidating size and dark, rough looks, and then she would have smiled politely and walked away from him.

Raven knew that Janna was a gift given to a lonely raven by the old Haida gods, the cruel gods who gave only that they might teach man the agony of loss by taking back the gift. Raven also knew that there was no way to fight the gods, no way to keep the gift and evade the agonizing loss. He could only cherish Janna for the time that she was his, and open his hands when the time was over, freeing her and praying that she would never regret having given herself for a time to a man she didn't love.

"You look as though someone carved you from stone," Janna murmured sleepily. Her fingertips traced the fierce lines on Raven's face, lines that faded even as he turned to kiss her palm. "What were you thinking about?"

"Eden and the old Haida gods," Raven said, smoothing his cheek into the warmth of Janna's hand. "And Eve." He lifted his head and looked at the gift of the gods lying within his arms. "You're so beautiful," he whispered. "All woman, hot and generous. A man could die trying to get enough of you." He sank his teeth into her palm with sensual precision. "And I can think of no better way to step into eternity than listening to your sweet cries."

Janna stared at Raven stretched out on the bed beside her, as naked and rugged as the mountains themselves.

Sunlight streamed through the porthole, pure light washing over his powerful body. He was so completely male, so very perfect in her eyes that she couldn't even speak to tell him how much it moved her to be desired by him. She could only touch him with a hand that trembled. The knowledge that she had pleased him gleamed in her eyes, tears shining in her lashes like distant stars. With a soft sound she went into the arms that opened for her in silent invitation.

"I love you, Raven," Janna said, holding him close. "I think I've loved you since the moment you pulled me out of the sea."

Raven closed his eyes as pain twisted through him. He kissed Janna very gently when she would have whispered her love again. Then he sealed Janna's lips with a long, callused finger.

"Don't," he whispered, looking at her silver-green eyes, wishing that she had never spoken. He had already guessed the source of any emotion she might have for him, the reason that he was set apart from other men in her eyes; he didn't need to be reminded that it was gratitude, not love, even when the reminder came in such a sweet and gentle way.

Janna stared at Raven, understanding only the pain in his bleak eyes, not the cause. "Raven?" she asked raggedly. "Don't you want—"

His lips came down over hers in a kiss that was as warm as sunlight and as powerful as the sea itself. He held her mouth for a long, long time, savoring her, wanting her.

"It's all right," Raven whispered finally against Janna's lips. "You don't have to love me. I know that you're grateful to be alive. I'm grateful, too. Without you I wouldn't have known what it was like to die inside you and then to live again with you inside me. I wouldn't have known what it was like to be in Eden, to find myself in a place out of time where no one exists but a single man and a single woman who were created for each other."

With a swift movement Raven took Janna's mouth. He felt a fierce elation when she opened willingly for the tender penetration of his tongue. He drank from her deeply and felt himself taken from in return before he lifted his head and looked down into eyes as enigmatic as mist veiling the primeval forest.

"Let's take this time, this savage Eden, this gift," Raven said huskily, kissing Janna between each word. "Take it without labels or promises that will haunt you when Eden is a memory and the rest of your life is very real. I want you to remember me with joy, for that's how I will remember you."

Janna closed her eyes and tried very hard not to cry out with the mingled pain and pleasure of being with the man she loved, a man who laughed with her and wept with her—and did not love her. Yet he made love to her as though she were the only woman on earth.

But she was not. There was one other woman for Raven. The woman he loved and could not have. Angel.

*Do you still love her?*

*Of course. And she loves me, too, now.*

Janna knew that she couldn't change that; she could only envy it. And she could take the bittersweet gift that was Raven, take him and understand that love was like Eden—savage, innocent, knowing only its own existence, its own needs, a law unto itself, a primeval island set in an endless sea of time.

"Yes," Janna whispered, holding on to Raven until she ached, giving him all of herself that he would allow.

"Yes, I want to be remembered with joy. Remember me, love. Remember that I loved you in a place out of time."

Raven tried to look into the green depths of Janna's eyes to the soul beneath, but he saw only the darkness of her long eyelashes and the silken swirl of her hair as her mouth caressed his chest. He started to speak but his breath caught. Her tongue was a dark, sweet flame burning over his skin and her cinnamon hair was wildfire caressing his arms.

He tried to slide his hands into her unbound hair. Before he could touch her, his whole body clenched and a hoarse sound was torn from his throat as her hands found his aroused flesh. She was woman and she was fire burning him all the way to his soul. With an inarticulate cry he found her softness, caressed her until she came to him and he could bury himself in her sweet, consuming fire, burning both of them alive.

The second time Janna woke up that morning, she was still locked within Raven's arms. She nuzzled the resilient chest hair that had been tickling her nose. He tightened his arms around her, silently telling her that he was awake. Smiling, she smoothed her cheek against his warm chest. Soundlessly she whispered *I love you* and accepted the stab of sadness that came with the knowledge that she wasn't loved in return. She was cherished, though, and enjoyed as a woman in a very elemental way. Every deliciously sensual ache in her body reminded her of that, as did her breast nestled warmly in Raven's big hand.

He might not love her, but he had given her a passion that grew greater each time they made love. For that alone, she would have stayed with him. When passion was joined with his gentleness and strength, his laughter and intelligence, Raven was revealed to her as the man she had always dreamed of and never truly believed she would find.

And she could not help hoping deep within her mind that any man who made love to her as Raven did could not be utterly lost to another woman. Surely Janna had a chance to steal his love with each kiss, each caress, each cry of ecstasy torn from him.

Janna nuzzled Raven again, realized that his flat nipple was within reach and touched it dreamily with the tip of her tongue. "Mmm. You taste good. Like an oyster. Salty."

"Want some lemon juice?"

"Raven on the half shell," Janna said, tasting him thoughtfully, then biting him with great care. "Nope. No lemon juice needed. Raw is best, the same way I found you."

Janna's stomach growled, reminding both of them that she had eaten nothing last night except a few oysters.

Smiling, Raven ran the ball of his thumb down her spine. "Want to flip to see who makes breakfast?"

"Heads," she said, then made a startled sound as she was picked up, turned over and gently placed face down on the bunk.

"Tails it is," Raven said, smoothing his palm over the supple curve of Janna's bottom. "Guess you lose. Unless you want to flip me for it, of course," he added innocently.

Janna pushed hair out of her eyes, saw Raven's wicked smile and realized, "I've been had."

"Several times," he agreed, laughing. He lifted Janna, pulled her slowly across his body and set her on her feet in the galley aisle. "And if you don't start breakfast soon," he added in a raspy voice as he nibbled on her thigh, "it's lunch we'll be flipping over." His tongue flicked out and he smiled as he heard her breath catch. "Or maybe dinner."

Janna's fingers threaded into Raven's black hair. When he caressed her again, she called his name in a husky voice that made him groan.

"What am I going to do with you?" he whispered. "Each time I have you I want you more."

She started to say something but all that came out was a tiny, wild sound as Raven's caresses became hotter, more intimate. "No more oysters for you," she said, biting her lip against a broken sound of pleasure.

Raven's breath washed over Janna's sensitive skin as he shook his head and nuzzled her at the same time. "If that legend were true," he murmured against her, "men would have hunted oysters to extinction long ago."

"Or women," retorted Janna.

He chuckled and nuzzled her soft flesh. "Are you saying that men would have hunted women to extinction, or women would have hunted oysters?"

"Precisely," Janna said. "I'm glad you understand. So many people are confused by a little straightforward ambiguity. What's for breakfast?"

He gave her body a look that made her knees weak.

"Raven," she breathed.

He closed his eyes. "I think I'll take a swim in the inlet while you cook tinned ham, potatoes and powdered eggs. After we eat you can take a shower while I clean up the galley. Then we'll go for a walk in the village while we still can."

"Still can?"

"Walk," Raven said succinctly. His eyes opened, and they glittered with sensual heat and laughter. "Didn't you know, small warrior?" he asked, his voice deep. "We're going to kill each other in bed." His teeth flashed whitely beneath the black mustache as he pulled the torn remains of Janna's nightshirt from the sheets. "Know something else?" he asked, dangling the ripped cloth from his fingertip. "I can hardly wait."

Janna bit her lower lip, caught between laughter and anticipation, self-consciousness and the breathtaking memory of the instant when Raven had first taken her. She knew that her expression must have revealed her thoughts, because Raven's eyes became heavy lidded and intent as he watched. With a small sound she grabbed the shredded T-shirt and hid her flushed face in it. She wasn't used to this kind of sensual teasing any more than she was used to making love—or being in love.

"I guess you're going to insist on wearing another of my T-shirts," Raven said gravely.

She nodded without looking up.

He smiled gently. "On one condition."

Warily, Janna lifted her head. "What's that?"

"The only thing you wear in bed is me."

Raven didn't ask whether the strangled sound Janna made was agreement or disagreement. He simply stood up, kissed her thoroughly, grabbed a bar of soap and vanished over the *Black Star*'s railing into the chilly inlet.

Somehow Janna had managed not to burn, spill or scatter the ingredients of breakfast when Raven emerged from the inlet after his saltwater bath. Naked, powerful, he looked perfectly at ease in the wild land. He also took Janna's breath away, made her hands shake and her heart beat violently. She wished that the storm were still churning beyond the inlet, locking them in, locking the world out.

Unfortunately, by the time breakfast was eaten and Janna had taken a shower, it was obvious that the storm was definitely over. She dressed gloomily, wishing that she weren't going to be kicked out of Eden quite so

quickly. She wondered if Raven had business waiting for
him, business that couldn't wait, or if perhaps he wouldn't
mind staying in Eden for a few days longer, giving her a
chance to steal just a little bit more of his love.

"Janna, I found it!"

She pulled another one of Raven's dark, huge T-shirts
over her head and called, "What?"

"A real sketchbook for you to use. I knew Angel
had left it around here somewhere, but I couldn't
remember where."

Janna zipped up her jeans and opened the door to the
cubicle that was both shower stall and head.

"Sketchbook?" Janna asked, pushing a curtain of
cinnamon hair aside. The thick, silky strands ignored
her fingers, falling forward again as soon as she lifted
her head. She pushed at the softly curling hair again,
trying to ignore the emptiness in the pit of her stomach
that came every time Angel's name was mentioned. "Is
Angel an artist?"

"One of the best," Raven said, smiling as he remembered the stunning stained glass panel that Angel had
done for his home on Vancouver Island. The panel
showed the *Black Moon*, his longline trawler, skimming
over a mysterious sea while salmon gathered below in
a seething silver storm. "Galleries are lined up begging
for her stained glass."

"Oh." Janna would have said more, but the thought
of competing for Raven with a woman who was not
only courageous, beautiful and blond but an artist, as
well, turned Janna's normally quick mind to glue. "Life
really isn't fair, is it?" she muttered under her breath.

"What?"

"Stained glass, huh?" Janna said, rallying her
thoughts with an effort, saying the first thing that came

# YOUR PARTICIPATION IS REQUESTED!

Dear Reader,

Since you are a lover of fiction – we would like to get to know you!

Inside you will find a short Reader's Survey. Sharing your answers with us will help our editorial staff understand who you are and what activities you enjoy.

To thank you for your participation, we would like to send you 2 books and a gift – **ABSOLUTELY FREE!**

Enjoy your gifts with our appreciation,

*Pam Powers*

**SEE INSIDE FOR READER'S SURVEY**

# What's Your Reading Pleasure...
## ROMANCE? _OR_ SUSPENSE?

Do you prefer spine-tingling page turners OR heart-stirring stories about love and relationships? Tell us which books you enjoy – and you'll get 2 FREE "ROMANCE" BOOKS or 2 FREE "SUSPENSE" BOOKS with no obligation to purchase anything.

Choose "ROMANCE" and get **2 FREE BOOKS** that will fuel your imagination with intensely moving stories about life, love and relationships.

**FREE!**

Choose "SUSPENSE" and you'll get **2 FREE BOOKS** that will thrill you with a spine-tingling blend of suspense and mystery.

**FREE!**

Whichever category you select, your 2 free books have a combined cover price of $11.98 or more in the U.S. and $13.98 or more in Canada.

And remember. . . just for accepting the Editor's Free Gift Offer, we'll send you 2 books and a gift, ABSOLUTELY FREE!

## YOURS FREE! We'll send you a fabulous surprise gift absolutely FREE, just for trying "Romance" or "Suspense"!

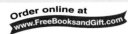

# YOUR READER'S SURVEY "THANK YOU" FREE GIFTS INCLUDE:

- ▶ 2 Romance OR 2 Suspense books
- ▶ A lovely surprise gift

**PLEASE FILL IN THE CIRCLES COMPLETELY TO RESPOND**

**1)** What type of fiction books do you enjoy reading? (Check all that apply)
- ○ Suspense/Thrillers   ○ Action/Adventure   ○ Modern-day Romances
- ○ Historical Romance   ○ Humour   ○ Science fiction

**2)** What attracted you most to the last fiction book you purchased on impulse?
- ○ The Title  ○ The Cover  ○ The Author  ○ The Story

**3)** What is usually the greatest influencer when you <u>plan</u> to buy a book?
- ○ Advertising   ○ Referral from a friend
- ○ Book Review   ○ Like the author

**4)** Approximately how many fiction books do you read in a year?
- ○ 1 to 6   ○ 7 to 19   ○ 20 or more

**5)** How often do you access the internet?
- ○ Daily  ○ Weekly  ○ Monthly  ○ Rarely or never

**6)** To which of the following age groups do you belong?
- ○ Under 18   ○ 18 to 34   ○ 35 to 64   ○ over 65

**YES!** I have completed the Reader's Survey. Please send me the 2 FREE books and gift for which I qualify. I understand that I am under no obligation to purchase any books, as explained on the back.

Check one:

| **ROMANCE** |
| 193 MDL EE3V   393 MDL EE37 |

| **SUSPENSE** |
| 192 MDL EE4K  392 MDL EE4V |

FIRST NAME          LAST NAME

ADDRESS

APT.#          CITY

STATE/PROV.          ZIP/POSTAL CODE

◄ DETACH AND MAIL CARD TODAY! ▶

(SUR-SS-06) © 1998 MIRA BOOKS

## The Reader Service — Here's How It Works:

Accepting your 2 free books and gift places you under no obligation to buy anything. You may keep the books and gift and return the shipping statement marked "cancel." If you do not cancel, about a month later we'll send you 3 additional books and bill you just $5.24 each in the U.S., or $5.74 each in Canada, plus 25¢ shipping & handling per book and applicable taxes if any.* That's the complete price and — compared to cover prices starting from $5.99 each in the U.S. and $6.99 each in Canada — it's quite a bargain! You may cancel at any time, but if you choose to continue, every month we'll send you 3 more books, which you may either purchase at the discount price or return to us and cancel your subscription.

*Terms and prices subject to change without notice. Sales tax applicable in N.Y. Canadian residents will be charged applicable provincial taxes and GST.

If offer card is missing write to: The Reader Service, 3010 Walden Ave., P.O. Box 1867, Buffalo, NY 14240-1867 to her tongue. "I saw a really gorgeous piece in a Seattle gallery last year. I wanted that panel so much I used to stand in front of it and just ache." The memory made Janna smile slightly at her own longing. "The glass reminded me of the Inside Passage at twilight, that magical time when all legends are true. There was rank upon rank of mountains falling away to the horizon in every shade of blue imaginable, and the sea was luminous, alive as only a god could be alive, breathing light and life into everything it touched. I wish to hell I could have afforded even a corner of that panel."

"Angel put a huge price on it because she couldn't bear to sell it," Raven said, smiling slightly. "It was one of her favorites."

"That was Angel's work?" Janna asked in disbelief.

Raven nodded. "She understands that the sea is the source of all life. She's a remarkable woman," he added, holding out the sketchbook to Janna. "Like you."

Janna didn't know whether to laugh or cry or scream at the sheer unfairness of it all. Bad enough to envy Angel Raven's love, but to admire her artistic skill as well was more than Janna's uncertain emotions could handle. Wordlessly she took the sketchbook and flipped through it. Only three of the pages had drawings on them, studies of driftwood on a wide, sandy beach. There was a balance of elements and a subtle elegance of line that tugged at Janna's senses, telling her of the artist's understanding of opposites and unity.

"I shouldn't use this," she said. "Angel might—"

"She wouldn't mind," Raven interrupted quickly. "These were just preliminary sketches. The finished piece was a gift to my grandfather."

Janna closed the sketchbook and looked at Raven with doubt in her silver-green eyes.

"Use it," Raven urged. "That way you won't have to go all the way to Masset and then all the way back here just to sketch the totems at dawn. Now that I've found a real sketchbook, you can stay a few days longer, can't you?" He stopped abruptly. "Unless you have to get back to Masset right away for some reason?"

Janna smoothed her fingers over the sketchbook while happiness made her eyes as luminous as the sea itself. "No," she said huskily, "I don't have to be anywhere at all. I'd like to spend a few more days in Eden. With you, Raven."

The pleased yet almost shy smile that Janna gave Raven made him reach for her and wrap her warmly in his arms. He inhaled her clean, womanly scent and closed his eyes, hardly able to believe his luck. A few more days in Eden.

And if his conscience gave him hell for taking advantage of Janna's gratitude, for keeping her away from the civilization that would take her from his arms as surely as night took the sun from the sky, then he would just point out to his conscience that it was only a few days, just a few, and Janna had so many thousands of days left in her life. Surely even after her feeling of gratitude wore off, she wouldn't look back and regret having spent those few extra days with a lonely raven.

"I found some pencils, too. Funny-looking ones," he said huskily. "Angel left them with the sketchbook. Want to see if they're the kind you need?"

"Sure," Janna said, holding Raven's big body until her arms ached, then reluctantly letting go.

The "funny looking" pencils turned out to be everything Janna would need to do finished drawings. She examined the pencils reverently, only to look up and see Raven watching her with an intensity that made her breath stop.

"You touch them as though they were magic," he said.

"They are," Janna said simply. "With them, I can draw. Without them, I'm a nightingale without a love song."

"In other words, a raven. Ravens sing love songs only in their dreams."

Janna hesitated, caught by the regret and acceptance that lay beneath Raven's words. "Then the raven's love song must be the most beautiful of all," she said softly, "for it's sung in silence."

Raven looked at her for a long moment before he smiled sadly. "You have the most beautiful eyes I've ever seen, Janna. Like the forest veiled in mist. Silver and green and radiant with life."

Not knowing what to say except *I love you*, the very words that Raven didn't want to hear, Janna smiled as sadly as he had. In silence he took the pencils from her and packed them carefully in a rucksack along with the sketchbook. She followed him to the makeshift dock. She was getting accustomed to the logs, but she still wasn't nearly as adept as Raven was. She was relieved to feel the rocky shore beneath her feet.

"There used to be paths here," Raven said.

He swept his broad hand in an arc across the shoreline. It was overgrown with salt-tolerant plants that crept above the tide line and blended into a mass of cedar, ferns and moss beds deeper than a mattress. After the first few steps Janna understood why the Haidas had depended on canoes rather than their feet for transportation.

Only where the ocean actually washed over the land could rock be seen. The rest of the inlet was covered in a seamless, multihued green blanket of life. If trees didn't grow in a given place, it was because the earth was too wet to support them. Boggy areas were

common. Even in the forest itself it was rare to see bare
bark or wood. Moss hung in beards and veils from every
surface. Deadfalls were draped in thick blankets of de-
ceptively solid-looking moss, making green traps that
waited to be sprung by unwary feet. Often trees grew
so close together that nothing could squeeze between.
Animal life abounded, but was nearly invisible—and
therefore safe from man. It was almost impossible to
hunt even something as large as a bear or a deer for the
simple reason that the hunter could see only a few feet
beyond the barrel of his rifle.

On the other hand, if the land were impenetrable, the
sea was not. Steep-sided inlets and deep sounds
provided natural shelter from storm and wind. Fish
abounded. Shellfish were always within reach. The
ancient Haidas had wisely taken the sea's gifts and used
only the narrow margin of land just beyond high tide
mark. It was there that they built their cedar lodges and
carved totem poles as tall as the tallest cedar trees. The
totems stood facing the sea, their weathered faces
bathed in the salt-laden wind. Raven identified the
highly stylized symbols for Janna, pointing out the
killer whale and the frog, the salmon and the eagle and
the raven with wings spread on top of the pole.

"What are you going to do while I sketch?" Janna
asked, pencil poised over pad.

"What I came here to do. Think."

She looked at Raven hastily, feeling guilty for having
interrupted him. He cupped his broad palm under her
chin and tipped her face up to his.

"I came here because I felt…restless. I don't feel that
way anymore." Raven brushed his lips over Janna's. "If
I didn't want to be here with you, we'd be on our way
to Masset right now. Go ahead and sketch all you want.

I'll be nearby if you need me." He started to walk away, then turned back. "Don't go into any of the old lodges. They're just waiting for an excuse to collapse."

"I won't," Janna said. She turned to look at the cedar houses slowly dissolving back into the land from which they had come. "The lodges belong to other people. It would be like trespassing."

"You mean you don't want to take them apart looking for beads and bones?" he asked sardonically.

Janna looked at Raven's impassive face. Slowly she shook her head. "There would be no point. I'm not an archaeologist. I can't recreate a lost past from a handful of fragments. So I'd rather just sit and sketch and let the ghosts whisper to me across the years."

Raven looked at Janna for a long moment, a look as consuming as any kiss he had ever given her. Then he touched her mouth with his fingertips, turned away and stepped into the forest.

He vanished.

Janna blinked, unable to believe that a man as big as Raven could disappear so quickly. She took several steps forward and saw the moss springing back into place where Raven's footsteps had compressed it. She took two more steps and stopped suddenly. Evergreens and moss surrounded her. There was no sky, no sea, no true ground, just the forest primeval enfolding her in a scented embrace. Even as she watched, the last evidence of Raven's passage vanished, leaving her utterly alone.

For a moment she stood without moving, caught by the elemental stillness of the forest. Then through the trees came the harsh, primitive cry of a raven searching for its mate. In the distance came a sound that could have been an answer. Janna held her breath, listening, but heard no more. The raven called again, farther away now, a shimmering black shadow skimming over endless shades of green.

After a few moments Janna turned and went toward the shore, knowing that if she attempted the forest alone she would be hopelessly lost within a few steps. There were no trails, no piled stones to point the way, no blazes old or new to mark the passage of man. She walked along the margin of land and sea. For a long time she stood wrapped in silence, looking at the massive icons of another time, another race, another culture, another way of looking at the complex mystery of life. She found totems that were canted, on the edge of toppling over, and totems that had fallen long ago. She found totems in which the cedar itself had somehow survived the carving and had taken root once more, sending out fragrant branches. The sight of faces watching her from between the lacy branches made the hair stir on Janna's neck, as though gods had come and taken root in the Queen Charlottes' savage Eden.

When Janna knew she could absorb no more of the emotional currents sweeping through and around her, she found a log that was thickly encrusted with moss, sat down and was soon lost in her sketches. Several hours passed before she looked up. Raven was back. She could sense his presence as surely as she had sensed that the Queen Charlottes were islands set apart from time. She looked over her shoulder and smiled. Raven's black eyes kindled in response.

"How long have you been there?" she asked.

"Long enough to admire your stillness, your concentration, your elegance," he said in a deep, soft voice. "You're like a doe listening for danger at the edge of the forest."

Janna's eyes widened to reveal silver-green depths.

She had never thought of herself as elegant or doelike. The realization that Raven saw those qualities in her was an immaterial caress shivering over her.

"Are you ready for a break?" Raven asked, glancing down at the sketch pad.

"My hand is numb," she admitted. "It's been a long time since I've drawn for that many hours. There's so much here, so many emotions, so little time to capture even the smallest echo of Eden…."

Raven took the pad and pencils from Janna and packed them carefully. "Follow me," he said, shouldering the rucksack. "I have something I want to show you."

She followed without question as he turned back to the forest that knew neither trail nor the possession of man. Within moments the sea was invisible, its sounds and scents lost. Nothing penetrated the mist-haunted silence but the distant cry of a raven.

"Stay in my footsteps," he cautioned. "We have to walk the edge of a small bog."

Soon the forest in front of them thinned dramatically, giving way to a clearing, where stunted evergreens struggled to maintain a toehold in land too wet to support them. The surface appeared solid, but Raven's footprints glistened with water squeezed from the humus by his weight. Water stood in small pools stained the color of tea by tannin leached from the surrounding forest. The water trickled away in small rills and rivulets until they came together in a creek. The water was absolutely clean, utterly unique in its amber clarity.

A small cabin stood just beyond the bog. The walls were of weathered cedar and the roof was finished with cedar shingles. Moss grew from every crevice between the shingles and clung to the walls. Yet the cabin was new rather than old; windows gleamed against the darker backdrop of the forest and the front door was finished with metal hinges.

"How did you find it?" Janna asked softly as she came up to stand beside Raven.

"I built it with my own hands."

She turned and looked at him. His eyes were very black, yet like the creek they were crystalline in their clarity. He was looking at the tiny cabin but he was seeing something else from his past, something that haunted him. His high cheekbones, straight nose and the powerful line of his jaw had never looked more solid, more elemental, a man carved from the enduring things of the earth.

"Come," Raven said quietly, turning to Janna and holding out his hand.

The hard warmth of Raven's palm sent a tremor through Janna. She laced her fingers deeply with his as he led her to the cabin. There was no lock on the door, no bolt, nothing to keep out intruders. In Eden there were no intruders, just one man and one woman and the land that knew no time.

Raven opened the door, lifted Janna into his arms and carried her into the shelter that he had built years ago. He left the door open, inviting in the fragrance of cedar and the unearthly radiance of mist-filtered light. There was little furniture in the room—a table, a chair, shelves that held shells and glass fishing floats that had drifted across the empty Pacific to be washed up on a distant shore. A fire was laid in a hearth that had been built from water-smoothed beach stones. Blankets had been folded to make a sleeping pallet close to the hearth.

"I would have brought you here sooner," Raven said as he kissed Janna's hair, "but there's only one room, only one place to sleep, and I was trying very hard to keep my hands off you." He smiled almost sadly. "I failed rather spectacularly, didn't I?"

"I'm glad," Janna said, pressing her lips against the corded muscles of his neck. "I love your hands on me, Raven."

His powerful arms flexed as he whispered her name, shifting her in his grasp until he could capture her mouth. The taste of him swept through her like a wind from the sea. She made a small sound at the back of her throat as she felt herself sliding over his hard body. With one arm he caught her hips against his own and moved slowly. She shivered and clung to his strength, knowing again the elemental pleasure of having him desire her.

Reluctantly Raven let Janna slide the rest of the way down his body until her feet touched the floor. He bit her lips in a series of tiny, hard kisses that made her breath break into a moan. When his tongue thrust slowly into her mouth she moved against him with sensual abandon. He groaned, let his mouth mate with hers for a wild moment, then lifted his head.

"No more," he said almost roughly.

"Why not?" Janna murmured, standing on tiptoe to kiss the pulse beating violently in Raven's throat.

"Because I promised myself that I would feed you first."

"What a lovely idea," she murmured, kicking out of her tennis shoes and stepping out of her jeans and panties with a few quick motions. "I thought you hadn't noticed that there were a few paragraphs you overlooked."

"Help," Raven said, but his smile said that the long, curving length of Janna's body was beautiful to him.

"You know," Janna said as she began to unbutton the big shirt that fit her like a dress.

Then she looked up and saw Raven's smile and decided that the shirt could wait. She would much rather touch him. With fingers that trembled she opened his flannel shirt, discovering the male textures of hair and hard muscle beneath.

"What paragraphs?" Raven persisted, though his pulse beat visibly, strongly, quickening with every touch of her mouth.

"That shelf of books that I read."

"Are you trying to tell me that last night I over-looked some paragraphs that intrigued you?" Raven's breath hissed in as Janna's tongue traced the flat disk of his nipple. He groaned when her teeth scraped delicately over him, bringing him to a hard point that she teased with her lips. "Did I miss something?" he asked hoarsely.

"Only the paragraphs dealing with ways to pleasure a man. An understandable oversight on your part," Janna added, smiling as she found and nuzzled Raven's other nipple into erect sensitivity. "After all," she pointed out reasonably, "I'm not a man."

Raven's big hand smoothed over her bare, silky hip and then tangled in the warm thatch of hair between her thighs. She was incredibly soft, hot, melting at his touch, and the knowledge that she wanted him as much as he wanted her made him feel heavy and very male.

"You're right," he said deeply, sliding his fingertips into Janna's utterly feminine heat. "You're definitely not a man," he groaned, loving her soft flesh with slow movements of his hand. "And I thank God for it."

Janna's fingers clenched on Raven's belt as she felt the first shimmering forerunners of ecstasy stream through her. Biting her lip against a moan, she tugged at the belt buckle until it opened. Beneath her fingers the warm metal buttons on Raven's jeans gave way with soft popping sounds.

"Janna…"

Raven's breath caught and his hips jerked reflexively against her caressing hands. His fingers closed over hers, preventing her from undressing him.

"Raven?" she asked softly, kissing the suddenly hot skin of his chest. "Don't you want me to touch you?"

He made a tearing sound that could have been laughter or a curse. "I'd die to have you touch me," he said roughly. "But if you take off my jeans, I'm going to open your legs and…" The words ended in a groan when Janna's fingers caressed Raven through the soft cotton of his underwear. "Don't undress me," he growled, dragging his open mouth across her forehead, her cheek, her lips, tasting her, needing her. "There are other ways I want to love you before I slide into you."

"Whatever you say," Janna murmured as she eased her fingers into the front opening of Raven's briefs.

She felt every muscle in his body tighten when she discovered and freed his erect flesh, bringing it into her caressing hands.

"Janna—"

"You're still dressed," she pointed out, slowly stroking Raven with hands that were both gentle and possessive, smiling at his hot response.

"You can get arrested for being 'dressed' like this," he retorted, stifling a groan of pure sensual pleasure as she rubbed slowly over him.

"There aren't any police in paradise," Janna said dreamily, absorbed in appreciating the results of her handiwork. When Raven didn't answer, she glanced up almost guiltily. His face was drawn, and his eyes were narrow black slits. "You don't mind being—"

"Looked at the way a cat looks at cream?" offered Raven.

His smile made Janna weak. "Is that how I'm looking at you?" she whispered.

"Yes," he said huskily. "And it makes me feel ten feet tall and as hard as the mountains."

"You are."

"Only with you," he said, shuddering heavily and thrusting between her palms. "Only with you."

With a harsh sound Raven buried one hand in Janna's thick auburn hair, pulling her head back until her body arched into his. With his other hand he began unbuttoning her shirt, but the sweet fire of her fingers kept distracting him.

"You're hell on my clothes," Raven rasped.

His arm flexed and the shirt parted beneath his big hand, sending buttons flying. He rubbed his palm across the hardened tip of Janna's breast until she called his name on a broken sound of pleasure. He caught the sensitive nipple between his fingers and tugged, smiling fiercely as she moaned.

"Come closer," Raven said, his voice so deep it was a growl. "Closer, small warrior. I'll show you another way to tease me. And you. Oh God, come closer!"

Raven's fingers shifted, sliding down Janna's body until he could rub lightly over the softness hidden between her legs. When she opened to invite a deeper touch he smiled and moved his hips suddenly, sliding his hot flesh between her legs. Her eyes widened with surprised and then became heavy-lidded with pleasure as his hips moved again. She held him more tightly against herself and moved her hips in turn, stroking him, watching him, enjoying the frank sensuality of his smile. Her fingers pressed him closer and then closer still, wanting more of him, needing him in a way that shook her.

"Raven, I…"

Janna's breath caught in a moan as she felt heat spreading out from her body, heat caressing Raven's male flesh, heat pleading for him to share it as it was meant to be shared…deeply. She opened her eyes and saw his face contorted as though he were in torment. She knew then that he wanted her so much that not taking her was agony for him. Instinctively she shifted, guiding him, pressing him into her softness. But that only increased the sweet agony, reminding them with every breath what it would be like to be completely joined.

Raven's eyes opened suddenly, utterly black, nearly wild with need. The pallet was across the room. It might as well have been across the world. He had to be inside Janna. He had to have her *now*. His arms closed around her with sudden, savage strength.

"Wrap your legs around me," he said, lifting her without warning. "Put your arms around my neck now and—yes—now!" he said hoarsely, thrusting into her welcoming body, feeling her close hotly around him.

Raven knew that his hands were probably bruising Janna with their powerful grip, but he couldn't force himself to let go. She was demanding him, every bit of him, with an abandon he could only fiercely enjoy. He drove into her again and again, watching her eyes haze with silver as she began to come apart in his arms. He felt the tiny ecstatic ripples deep within her body, the spreading satin heat of her response, and he savored her nails pricking him with each sweet cry that was torn from her lips. He fought to control himself but it was impossible, the pleasure he felt was too savage, too deep, pulse after pulse of ecstasy pouring out of him, shaking him to his soul.

Janna closed her eyes and rested her head on Raven's powerful shoulder as she whispered her love too softly for him to hear.

But he did hear. He spoke her name in the silence of his mind, apologizing for keeping her in his savage Eden, promising to release her in just one more day, giving her back to her own life. Just one more day, one among thousands.

*I think I've loved you since the moment you pulled me out of the sea.*

Raven brushed his lips over Janna's hair and wished bitterly that gratitude were another name for love.

# Chapter 8

Janna watched the harbor at Masset slide closer with every instant. Futilely she wished that the *Black Star*'s engines would fail or that the storm could have lasted a few more days, a few more weeks, forever. But that was a dream. Reality was Raven guiding the boat smoothly to a rest against the commercial dock to fill up on fuel. Reality was the fact that Raven had said nothing to her about seeing her again after she walked off the boat. Reality was a numbness spreading through Janna's soul, freezing her.

Raven glanced at Janna and then quickly looked away. The closer they had come to Masset, the more she had retreated from him. He wasn't surprised by her withdrawal, but he was surprised by the tearing pain that he felt because of it. He had known nothing like it, even when Angel had turned on him in her rage and her despair. He wanted to go to Janna and hold her close against his body, to hear her words of love just once more. The temptation was almost overwhelming.

Grimly Raven flexed his hands on the wheel, relaxing them. It was bad enough that he had taken Janna when she would have been vulnerable to any man. If he prolonged his own pleasure at her expense any longer, he wouldn't be able to meet his own eyes in the shaving mirror.

"Want 'em topped, Raven?" called the lanky boy running the pumps.

Raven waved his agreement without looking up.

Because it hurt too much to watch Raven, Janna turned her attention to the boy. He had black hair and dark brown eyes and a promise of future power in his long body. Janna noticed his confidence as he tied off the boat and wondered if Raven had looked like that as a teenager. The realization that she would never know was another kind of pain lancing through her.

"You seen Uncle yet?" asked the boy.

"No," Raven said, vaulting easily up onto the dock. Other men hailed him. He waved in answer, but didn't look away from the boy. "Did he want me for something? Is that gallery agent holding up payment again?"

Raven's voice sounded unusually deep, impossibly resonant, carrying across the water like the tone of a perfectly cast bell. For the first time in days Janna was conscious of Raven's sheer size. He was literally head and shoulders above the men around him. Yet to her it was the other men who looked wrong, different, out of place, unreal. Raven had become the standard against which she measured others. The realization shocked her.

"Nah," the boy muttered, jiggling the nozzle against the boat. "That agent ain't said nothing but yessir and nosir since you told him there was plenty of white galleries that'd take Uncle's carvings, pay him on time and kiss his Indian ass in the bargain."

Janna saw Raven's razor smile and realized that although he had always cherished her, even at the times of his greatest need, there was a core of cold savagery in him—and that he used it to protect those he loved.

"Glad to hear it," Raven said with satisfaction. "What's the problem, then?"

"Uncle says he's falling in love and it's all your fault." Strong white teeth gleamed in the boy's tanned face.

"Oh?" Raven grumbled. "What have I done now?"

The boy jerked his chin in the direction of the land. "You left her in Uncle's lap while she was waiting for you to get back from Totem Inlet."

Janna saw Raven turn and look up the dock toward land. Suddenly his face was transformed, all darkness gone, a broad smile flashing as he held out his arms. The slender blonde who had been sneaking down the dock to surprise Raven laughed and ran toward him openly, throwing herself into his arms with the confidence of a woman who knows she will be caught and held securely. Raven's big arms closed around her, and he whirled around and around on the dock while the woman laughed joyously and clung to him.

Feeling as though she were being spun around herself, Janna swayed and then leaned against the cabin wall, wondering where all her strength had gone. She could barely stand. Only then did she admit to herself how much she had hoped that a man as passionately and wildly aroused as Raven had been when they made love must have been at least a little bit involved with his emotions as well as his body.

*Oh, he's in love, all right,* Janna admitted to herself.

*But not with me. I was just a temporary Eve in Raven's own savage Eden.*

Janna looked away from the slender, elegant blonde who was only now being set down on feet shod in Italian leather sandals. Glumly Janna looked at her own feet. They were covered by tennis shoes that were cracked from repeated bouts with salt water and the galley oven. The unflattering comparisons didn't stop there, either. Instead of wearing a clingy sea-green sweater, her own body was draped in an oversize man's shirt whose sleeves kept coming unrolled over her knuckles. Instead of smooth, scented hands, her own were chapped by seawater and covered by various nicks and welts that had come from wrestling with stubborn oyster shells.

No wonder Raven had only wanted a few days with her. Lord, the wonder was that he had wanted her at all. He must have been alone in that inlet for months to even look at her, much less to make love to her as though she were the last woman on earth—or the first.

*Finished feeling sorry for yourself yet?* Janna inquired sardonically of her frazzled reflection in the cabin window.

*No. I'm just getting started. Try me in a few years. I might be finished by then.*

*I can't wait. Quit complaining and pull up your socks.*

*I'm not wearing socks.*

*Pull them up anyway.*

Janna closed her eyes, rested her forehead against the cold glass and remembered all the times she had pulled up her socks and gotten on with life even when it hurt to breathe. She had no right to complain about the fact that Raven loved a woman he couldn't have and didn't love Janna, who loved him. Raven didn't love her, but he had given her the gift of himself for a few days. She had known what it was like to see a man's eyes kindle with laughter and desire as he watched her. She had known what it was like to evoke a fierce, elemental response from Raven's powerful body, to pleasure him and to be pleasured in turn.

She should be on her knees right now thanking him rather than trying not to cry because a few days weren't a lifetime. Nobody had promised her a lifetime. Nobody had promised her a damn thing. She could have died before she had ever known Raven.

She almost had.

"Are you all right?"

Janna's eyes flew open. The voice was deep, but not as deep as Raven's. The boat dipped beneath the man's weight as he came aboard. He was tall, but not as tall as Raven. He was strong, but he didn't have Raven's unusually powerful build. His hair was just as black, though, and in a lean, hard way he was as handsome as any man Janna had ever seen.

"Hawk," Janna said, remembering Raven's description of the man Angel loved. *Handsome as sin.*

A black eyebrow arched in silent query, giving an almost satanic cast to Hawk's face. His eyes were an odd shade of golden brown, like whiskey or the bird of prey he took his nickname from. "Have we met?"

"Only in a Raven's mind."

"A raven? Oh, Carlson." Hawk's mouth curled up slightly beneath a black mustache as he looked at Janna wrapped so intriguingly in what was obviously not her shirt. The mismatch between the shirt's size and her own had the effect of emphasizing how different her body was from a man's. "Leave it to Carlson to go out fishing and come back with a stunning mermaid."

Janna's mouth turned down in a sad curve. She felt more stunned than stunning.

"Are you sure you're all right?" Hawk asked gently.

"Sure. Just pulling up my socks."

"You aren't wearing any."

"Yeah. That's where the real challenge comes in."

Hawk smiled suddenly.

Janna blinked. She had never seen a smile quite so unexpected, like a fire burning beneath glacial ice, a promise of warmth radiating magically through the cold.

"My God," Janna said, shaking her head, "I'll bet when you and Raven walk down a street together you can hear female hearts breaking like dropped crockery."

There was an instant of startled stillness before Hawk's smile became a warm male laugh that was every bit as unexpected and as beautiful as his smile had been.

Raven turned toward the sound, still holding Angel. "I see you've met Janna," he said, grinning. "She has the most incredible—"

"Sense of humor," Janna interrupted wearily. "With that and two quarters you can get a cup of coffee."

Raven's eyes narrowed at the flatness he heard in Janna's voice. It reminded him painfully of the night when she had fled his heavy-handed company and locked herself in the bow to sketch. Janna didn't see his sudden scrutiny as she pushed away from the cabin's support.

"Do you need to get anything from the boat?" Hawk asked, looking between Janna and Raven with barely concealed curiosity.

She drew a deep breath, grabbed the tops of her non-existent socks and pulled. "Not a thing," she said with forced cheer. "That's one of the joys of shipwreck—no excess baggage. No baggage of any kind, as a matter of fact. What you see is what you get."

An arched black eyebrow lifted in query again but Hawk said nothing. Enviously Janna watched as he mounted the dock in a single lithe movement. The gap between boat and dock looked enormous to her. She was certain that she would stumble and go sprawling, further separating herself in Raven's eyes from the ever-perfect, ever-unattainable Angel.

"Let me help."

Startled, Janna looked up into compassionate golden-brown eyes. She held up her arms and was lifted onto the dock as gracefully as though she were a prima ballerina.

"Thanks," she said. "With my luck I'd have taken a header into the bay."

Janna's glance slid past Hawk to where Raven and Angel stood arm in arm. Suddenly a swim in the bay seemed preferable to walking down the dock and smiling cheerfully as she said goodbye to the man she loved.

"Rough trip?" Hawk asked, following the direction of Janna's glance.

"Yeah, you could say that. Lost my boat, lost my engine, lost my camping gear, my sketchbook, my…"

"Heart," finished Hawk too softly for anyone but Janna to hear.

Her mouth flattened into a line of pain. Those odd-colored eyes saw far too much.

"An overrated organ," Janna said, shrugging. "The body seems to function quite well without it."

Hawk started to say something. Janna cut him off with an overly bright smile and a rush of words.

"I'm sure the three of you have a lot to catch up on,"

she said firmly. "Tell Raven that I'll leave his shirt with the gas jockey."

"Why don't you tell me yourself?" Raven asked, walking up in time to overhear Janna's words.

His voice was very deep, almost harsh. He saw Angel's swift, assessing look in his direction and realized that he wasn't concealing his anger very well. But he hadn't expected to look up and see Janna nestled trustingly between Hawk's hands, to see her watching Hawk's face as though she expected a second sunrise to take place there at any moment.

Nor had Raven expected Janna to vanish from his life without so much as a word. He had known that gratitude was a fleeting emotion, yet the idea that Janna could walk away from the past few days as though they had never happened enraged him. Before he realized what he was doing, Raven found himself pressing Janna in exactly the way that he had promised himself he wouldn't.

"You can give me the shirt tomorrow, when I pick you up," he said to Janna, and his tone said that he wouldn't take no for an answer.

"Pick me up," Janna repeated numbly, feeling her heart turn over as she tried desperately not to hope that Raven was reluctant to let her go.

"For a picnic on a north-facing beach. If it's clear. Very clear. Otherwise any beach will do," he added.

"Very clear," she said, when it was anything but.

"Right. That's the only time you can really see the illusions."

Janna took a deep breath. "Help."

The hard lines left Raven's face as he smiled. His hand snaked out, wrapped around the nape of Janna's neck and gently pulled her close, disengaging her from Hawk's grasp in the process.

"I'm glad you remembered what I'm good for," Raven growled.

"Help?"

"Among other things."

"Oh help," Janna breathed raggedly, feeling herself go soft in the head and everywhere else at the feel of Raven's big, warm hand on her sensitive nape. "You're making it very hard for me to be noble," she said, speaking before she thought. She winced. Not thinking before she spoke was a chronic condition for her around Raven.

"Noble?" he asked, his black eyes searching her face.

"I…I thought you might want to get on with the, uh, reunion without any…any outsiders to get in the way."

Raven said something succinct and harsh under his breath. "If there's anything that gives me a tired butt, it's nobility," he added, ignoring the fact that his anti-nobility statement was self-serving. Nobility required him to give up Janna right away. Suddenly he was damned if he were going to do that. She had a few more days in the Queen Charlottes before she had to go back to Seattle. There wasn't one reason on earth they couldn't spend those days together. A lot of reasons why they *shouldn't*, but none why they *couldn't*. "Unless you're too behind in your sketching to take the time to spend a few days sight-seeing with me?"

For an instant Janna closed her eyes, unable to bear the dark clarity of Raven's eyes looking at her, into her, seeing too much. Just as she was seeing too much. Whatever else Raven might feel for Angel, there was no deep, reckless current of desire beneath his obvious love for her. Yet Janna knew that Raven was capable of intense sensuality and white-hot, elemental desire, for she had been the focus of both. Raven didn't love Janna, but he wanted her.

And she wanted him in the same way. If the savage, shimmering wine of sensual ecstasy was all that he could accept from Janna, then she wouldn't withhold it. She couldn't. She loved him too much to deny him anything.

Janna didn't notice the two other people watching her—Hawk with compassion and Angel with growing surprise and delight. Janna saw only Raven, the man she had waited a lifetime to find.

And to lose.

But not yet. She had a few days left in this wild Eden. She would spend them with the man she loved.

"I don't need to sketch anymore," she said, her tone husky. "I found everything I needed in Totem Inlet." The words came back to Janna, haunting her with too many meanings. "For my work," she added quickly, tearing her glance away from Raven's. "Thanks to Angel."

"Your sketchbook," Raven explained to Angel without looking away from Janna.

Angel blinked her beautiful sea-green eyes at him, turned toward Hawk and said, "Must be those Tlingit shaman genes shorting out the brain again."

"Tlingit?" Janna asked, not looking away from Raven. "I thought you were Haida."

"Mostly. One of my grandparents was a Tlingit shaman. Angel says that's where I get my fishing luck and streak of cruelty."

"Carlson!" Angel said, dismayed. "That's not what I said and you know it!"

Janna looked at Raven's off-center smile and wanted to cry. "You're not cruel," she said.

"Oh, but I am," he countered softly, his eyes bleak. "Remember? Sometimes comfort just doesn't get the job done."

"That's not cruelty, that's just a very difficult way to be kind," Angel said, putting her hand on the thick muscle of Raven's forearm. "If you had enjoyed my pain, then it would have been cruelty. Just because I was too selfish to see your kindness at the time doesn't change reality. You helped me, Raven." She laughed suddenly, a sound that was surprisingly sad. "You did more than help me. Without you I wouldn't have made it."

Raven hesitated, then picked up Angel's hand, kissed it softly and replaced it on his arm. "I'm glad you feel that way, Angel Eyes. I hated hurting you."

"It was nothing to what I did to you. If you only knew how many times I've regretted what I said to you." Angel took a deep breath and let it out slowly. She turned toward Janna and smiled apologetically. "You must think we're all crazy."

"No," Janna said quietly. "I think that Raven is very good at saving lives, at being kind even when it hurts, at being…a man. More man than I've ever met."

She clasped her hands together and hoped no one could see that her fingers were shaking from the reaction that had come when Raven had picked Angel's hand up and kissed it so gently, so sadly. Seeing Raven with the woman he loved and couldn't have was tearing at Janna in ways that she would never have expected. It wasn't just herself that she was hurting for. It was Raven.

"He saved my life, too," Janna continued in a tight, desperately calm tone. "And he won't even let me thank him."

"Gratitude is like milk," Raven said roughly. "It's bland, coats your tongue and turns sour after a few days." He turned toward the boy who was manning the fuel pump. "You finished yet?"

"Gettin' there."

"Good," Raven growled, impatient to be off the dock. "Where do you live?" he asked, turning back to Janna.

"In a small house on the beach at the edge of the park."

Raven frowned. "The shack with the bear feet hanging on the mailbox?"

"Is that what they are? I was pretty sure, but I was afraid to ask." Janna shuddered, remembering her horror when she had encountered the mailbox in the twilight rain. "The first time I saw them I thought they were bare feet as in no shoes, no socks, nothing but bones. Human. There was no reason to think otherwise. The claws had been cut off, and the articulation of the foot bones and ankle looked just the same as I remembered from my anatomy class. I nearly turned around and ran for the RCMP."

Almost reluctantly, Raven grinned. "You wouldn't have been the first. The Mounties had a bad summer a few years back. Someone shot several bears, took the claws and skin and dragged the carcasses out to sea. The beachcombers who found the feet washed up with rope around the ankles felt the same way about it that you did. So did the Mounties until they figured out what had happened." His smile faded. "Nadine has a grisly sense of humor. Has she fixed up that shack you're renting?"

"It only leaks when it rains," Janna said, shrugging.

"Like the boat," retorted Raven. "It only leaked when it was floating. Now it doesn't leak at all."

Raven's narrowed eyes told Janna that he disapproved of her summer lodging. Well, there was nothing she could do about that. The price had been right and had included the use of a boat and an outboard engine. Unfortunately, both boat and engine were at the bottom of Totem Inlet.

"Know any place to buy a used boat?" Janna asked, then added hastily, "Cheap."

"I'll take care of it," Raven said. "Old Nadine has gouged her last tourist."

"That isn't necessary. I can—"

"Care to flip me for it?" Raven interrupted smoothly.

Janna started to argue, took one look at the suddenly hard lines on Raven's face and decided that now wasn't the time to object. She had discovered that every time she mentioned Nadine's boat, Raven lost his sense of humor. Janna knew why. He kept thinking that if he had slept harder or started out to help later or never been at the inlet at all, Janna would have drowned.

The same thought had occurred to Janna more than once, usually in the small hours of the night, bringing her awake with her heart pounding. It had been very reassuring to feel Raven's warm presence by her side at those moments, to curl against his body as he gathered her close, to fall asleep knowing that she was safe.

"No, I don't care to flip you for it," Janna admitted, smiling slightly. "You use the damnedest coins."

Raven smiled in return, remembering both Janna's startled look and the creamy curves of her bottom as he had stroked it. "That leaves dinner to settle." He turned toward Hawk. "You two staying with Uncle?"

"He wouldn't hear of anything else."

"I'll bet. Uncle has an eye for beauty. Better keep Angel on a short leash. Uncle's quite the lady's man."

Hawk's mouth curved in a small smile. "Handsome devil, too. It's not hard to see where you got your pretty face."

Angel burst out laughing. "Hawk, you ought to be ashamed. Uncle is as homely as a muddy clam and you know it. Raven definitely is *not*."

"He's too small for my taste," Hawk said blandly.

Raven chuckled as he stepped forward and enveloped Hawk in the kind of hard hug that men reserve for brothers or the rare unrelated male whose friendship is uniquely valued. "I've missed you, Hawk. I'm glad you could get away for a few days."

"So am I. We don't see much of you in Vancouver anymore."

"I've been—restless."

"Yes," Hawk said softly. "I was restless, too. Once." He looked at Angel. "But no more."

Angel looked up at Hawk and smiled.

If Janna had had any lingering question about Raven's status in Angel's life, that doubt vanished. Angel's smile said silently that Hawk was as deeply rooted in her as her own soul. It was the same for Hawk. The single caressing touch of his fingertip on Angel's cheek proclaimed that she was a radiance that illuminated every darkness he had ever known.

Janna looked at Raven and saw his gentle smile as he watched the almost tangible currents of love flowing between his friends. Abruptly a feeling of sadness swept over Janna, a strange, almost overwhelming compassion for Raven. Angel and Hawk were two halves of a very beautiful, very powerful whole. Raven not only accepted that, he celebrated it, loving both of them equally, enjoying the visible evidence of their love for one another.

*I'm not that generous,* Janna realized bleakly. *I don't begrudge what Angel and Hawk have with each other— but I can't help wanting that kind of love for myself, too. Wanting it until I feel as though I've been turned inside out, every torn nerve exposed to salt air. Wanting it until I can't trust myself to look at Raven and not cry for me, for us.*

*For him.*

*Because I want it for him, too. Even if it doesn't happen with me, I want him to have that kind of love, too. I want it even more than I want it for myself. And I can't help him any more than I can help myself.*

"Janna? What's wrong?" Raven whispered.

Slowly Janna realized that she was leaning against Raven's hard, warm chest and his arm was unobtrusively supporting her.

"Nothing new," she said, looking up, giving him the best smile she had at the moment. It must not have been very good. His eyes narrowed and he looked at her closely. "I guess it's all catching up with me," she said, waving her hand around vaguely. "Coping with civilization and all that. Eden was…addictive."

Raven's eyes kindled. His arms tightened around Janna. "It doesn't have to end," he whispered. He took a harsh breath as he heard his own words. He was doing what he had promised he wouldn't, pressing her, using her gratitude for his own ends. "You have a few more days, don't you? If you want?"

"I want," Janna whispered, giving in to the need within her soul and holding on to Raven suddenly. "I want that very much."

Both of Raven's arms went around Janna. He straightened slowly, lifting her feet off the dock, loving the feel of her completely supported within his arms. When he finally set her down again, he was aware of Angel's amused, approving smile.

"It's settled," Raven said. "We'll meet for dinner at Janna's place at five. I'll bring the food, Angel will cook and Hawk will clean up afterward."

"That doesn't leave anything for me to do," Janna pointed out.

"You," Raven said, touching her nose with his big finger, "are sentenced to a long, hot bath. Then you will sit in my lap and whisper to me about the lives and lusts of frumious bandersnatches."

"I don't think you're old enough to hear stuff like this," Hawk said, covering Angel's ears with his hands.

"Dream on," she retorted, covering Hawk's ears with her own small hands and then tugging gently, bring his face down to hers. She whispered something that made his eyebrows climb and then he laughed out loud.

"You're on," he said, smiling down at her with sensual promise.

Janna had just finished undergoing the first part of her "sentence" when she heard a knock on the front door.

"Is that you, Raven?" she called out, reaching for a towel.

"In the flesh," he said, walking in the front door and shutting it behind him. "How about you? What are you in?"

"The same. Period. Are you early or am I late?" she asked, peeking around the barely opened bathroom door.

Raven smiled as he nudged the door fully open. "I'd say I was just in time."

The breath caught in Janna's throat when she saw Raven's slow, sensual appraisal of her body.

"God," he said thickly, "you're too beautiful to be real."

The visible shivers that coursed over Janna's skin were the result of more than the cooler air coming into the steamy bathroom.

"Raven," she said huskily, but could say no more.

"Again," he murmured.

"What?"

"My name."

Raven's voice was so deep that Janna almost couldn't understand the words. He bent over her, tasting her flushed skin with slow, sensual movements of his tongue.

"Raven," Janna said. She tried to say his name again, but his mouth was teasing her breast into a hard ruby peak. The contrast of his hair against her skin was like black satin against pearl. "Raven," she said, trembling and threading her fingers into his hair as he knelt before her.

"Yes," he growled softly against the taut curve of her belly. "Like that. Say it like that. Say it as though it were the only word in the only language that mattered."

Janna felt the firm caress of Raven's hands as he stroked her body from her high-arched feet to her rounded hips, memorizing her. His tongue traced a hot, sensuous line from her knee to the nest of dark hair at the apex of her thighs, drawing tiny gasps and cries from her, making heat swirl through her in a glittering diamond mist.

"Raven," Janna said raggedly, feeling his tongue in slow, honeyed caresses that unraveled her. *"Raven."*

"Yes," he said as triumph flared heavily through him. "Like that. Call my name while I love you. When you say it like that it makes me want—everything. With you. Here. Now. Forever."

Janna clung to Raven and called his name in a husky, helpless litany of love while he cherished her. When she could no longer stand he lifted her in his arms and carried her to the small bedroom. Very gently he put her on the dark bedspread and then simply stood next to her, his clear black eyes watching her flushed body as though he had never seen a woman before.

"Raven?" she asked in a trembling voice.

Without looking away from Janna, Raven began to undress. "I'm going to love you," he said deeply. "I'm going to love you until I'm the only thing in the world to you, until my name is the only word you can remember, until you're crying for me with every breath you take. I'm going to watch your eyes change to silver when I slide into you and you come apart beneath me. Then I'm going to lick the tears from your face and begin all over again."

The hot, nearly savage certainty in Raven's eyes was reflected in his hard flesh as he knelt over her, touching her, loving her. Janna tried to speak but could not, for her body had been taken from her at his first intimate caress. She tried to speak again, but all that came out was a primitive sound of pleasure that made him smile.

And then the only sound in the room was Janna's voice calling his name in a husky, helpless love song for the raven who did not love her in return.

## Chapter 9

On the last day of August Janna awoke slowly, rubbing her cheek against the resilient wall of muscle that was Raven's chest. He made a sound of sleepy contentment, cuddled her even closer and fell back asleep between one breath and the next. Janna nuzzled Raven's warm skin contentedly but didn't go back to sleep herself. She hadn't wanted to sleep at all last night after they had come back from their trip to the Yakoon River. She hadn't wanted to waste a single instant of what might be her last hours with Raven.

Today she was going to tell him that she loved him. Today she hoped that he would accept her love rather than tenderly denying it. Today he would either love her in return or she would have to leave—for Janna knew if she stayed any longer with Raven she wouldn't be able to leave him. She wasn't even sure that she could go now. She only knew that she had to try. She loved

Raven far too much to burden him with a woman and an emotion that he didn't want.

*Surely he loves me, if only a little,* Janna thought, pressing her cheek into Raven's abundant warmth. *No man who didn't love just a little could be so gentle, so passionate, so pleased just to be with me.*

Raven made no secret of his pleasure in Janna's company. Even though she had pointed out that Angel and Hawk had come to the Queen Charlottes to see Raven, not a strange woman, he had ignored Janna's protests. He was rarely beyond her reach and was never beyond the sound of her voice. She fell asleep with the taste of him on her lips and the warmth of him within her, and she awoke to the feel of his heartbeat beneath her cheek and the heat of his body pressed full-length against hers.

She had sat in Raven's lap and whispered frumious nonsense in his ear and had heard his deep laughter mingling with her own. She had gone to the legendary Tlell River and seen fishermen pull shining salmon from whiskey-colored water that was as clear and wild as a hawk's eyes. She had seen gusts of wind swirl over river and sea, brushing the water's surface with quick-silver designs. She had heard gulls wheel and keen on the leading edge of a storm, birds crying their need to the careless sky. She had stood on the banks of the Yakoon River and seen a spruce tree burning like a golden flame against the primeval green of the forest. There was no other tree of its kind on earth. Not one. Unique, alone, living in an untamed Eden. Janna had wept to see Raven and the golden spruce together, their power and their isolation complete.

And always, always, whether on the sea or in the forest, Janna had sensed in the primal silence the returning echoes of a raven's lonely cry.

She knew only one way to reach into that isolation, to answer that searching cry. Yet each time she had tried to tell Raven of her love he had taken the words from her lips, the breath from her body and he had substituted his own sensual words, his own breath in her body until he became part of her once more and she could say only his name, feel only his power within her, know only him and the elemental ecstasy he brought to her.

The thought that she might never again know that shimmering flight in Raven's arms made Janna close her eyes in silent pain. With a deep, slow breath she fought back the sadness, for she had promised herself that this day would be as perfect as she could make it. There would be no tears, no wounded dreams crying to be made whole. There would be only laughter and companionship and the haunting, bittersweet beauty of one final day in Eden.

And at the end of that day she would tell Raven that she loved him. At the end of that day she would know whether he loved her in return.

Janna kissed the muscular warmth of Raven's chest, nuzzling the vaguely curly wedge of hair that tickled her nose. She discovered the dark disk of his nipple just within reach of her tongue. She circled the sensitive flesh, enjoying the taste and texture of Raven. It was delicious to have him all to herself, to slowly awaken him as he had always awakened her—deep within the hot, silken web of his sensuality, fully aroused by erotic sensations that were both dreamlike and very real, flying even higher as he merged with her and brought her the ecstasy that came only on the glittering black wings of a wild raven.

Now it was Janna's turn to savor the sleeping power of the man she loved. She might never have another chance to awaken Raven with slow, hot caresses. She might never again know the pleasure of bringing him from sleep into ecstasy.

Janna eased aside the bedcovers and looked at Raven's naked, beautifully masculine body. She knelt over him as her fingertips smoothed each ridge and swell of muscle, her touch soothing, encouraging him to remain within his dreams. He shifted beneath her caresses, responding even in his sleep, moving closer to the warm hands stroking him. Smiling, wondering what his dreams were like at the moment, Janna tasted Raven's skin with slow, catlike touches of her tongue while her palms savored the heat and muscular lines of his torso. As she nibbled and softly nipped her way from his chin to his hips, she sensed him awakening. The tip of her tongue circled his navel and then filled it with hot, delicate caresses.

Beneath Janna's hands Raven's thighs were hard, corded with muscle, powerful even when relaxed. The dense thatch of hair that lay between was an irresistible lure to her. She eased her fingers into it, seeking and finding all the changing textures of his masculinity. The differences between his body and her own fascinated her. She cherished those differences with her fingertips, her palms, her hands holding and caressing him as he changed to meet her touch. His potency compelled her in an elemental way. She wanted to know him with the same searing, wild intimacy with which he had known her.

"You're fishing in rocky waters again," Raven rumbled, his tone both amused and thick with arousal.

"Yes," Janna said, cradling his very different flesh in her hands, "I know. This time, I know."

Raven smiled as he remembered the first time they had awakened in bed together, when Janna hadn't recognized the distinctive male flesh rising hard and hot beneath her hand.

"I want to...touch you," she said softly, caressing him. "Do you mind?"

"Do I look like I mind?" he asked, his voice gritty.

Janna looked from the heavy-lidded sensuality of Raven's eyes to the hard flesh that she was caressing. "No," she agreed huskily, "You don't look like you mind. But there are other ways of touching, ways that appalled me before I knew you." She smiled slightly, thinking of that shelf of books she had thrown away after her divorce. "There are whole chapters I want to explore. With you, Raven. Only with you. Would you mind that?"

She felt the sudden, savage tightening of his body as he understood what she was asking.

"Whatever you want, small warrior," Raven said, his voice dark, caressing, thick with anticipation. "However you want it."

"'For as long as you can take it,'" Janna added, smiling, remembering what Raven had once said to her. "I'm glad you're an unusually strong man," she whispered, bending down to him. "Very glad."

The long, wide beach uncurled in front of Raven and Janna like an immense ribbon. The wind that had swept away clouds and mist alike had also stirred the ocean into a dark blue mass where whitecaps flashed and vanished only to reform again atop other metallic blue swells. Lines of breakers rolled toward the beach in creamy ranks, adding a rhythmic thunder to the deep baying of the wind. Neither picnic tables nor trash cans marred the sand's pristine surface. There were no footprints, no people, nothing but the wind and the sea and the distant keening of gulls.

"I feel as though I'm trespassing," Janna said, looking behind at the tracks they were leaving in the sand.

"The tide will wash it clean again," Raven said. "It will be as though we were never here." He looked at the position of the sun in the sky. "We have some time before Angel and Hawk are meeting us. Want to explore?"

Raven caught the sensual, almost secret smile that came to Janna's lips and didn't know whether to laugh or swear at the sudden hot rush of his blood.

"I was referring to exploring the beach," Raven continued, "but I'm open to suggestion." Knowing he shouldn't, unable to stop himself, he bent and kissed Janna slowly, savoring the taste and textures of her mouth. "In fact," he said, unzipping her wind shell and sliding his hand up beneath her sweater, "I've got a few suggestions of my own."

Janna threaded her fingers deeply into Raven's hair. "You know," she said, biting his lower lip with sensual precision, "I ought to call your bluff. Because after this morning, bluff is all it could be!"

"Wanna bet?" he asked, smiling darkly.

Raven knew he should release Janna from the net of his sensuality. That was why he had come to the beach of illusions—to let her go. Yet his free hand was even now caressing her buttocks, kneading the firm flesh as he pressed her body tightly against him.

Janna's breath came in swiftly. Raven was as hard and ready as though they hadn't just spent the morning hours exploring his strength and endurance.

"Yeah," Raven said, smiling oddly when he saw Janna's expression change. He moved his hand up to caress a velvety nipple that hardened beneath his fingers. "It's the damnedest thing," he admitted. "I never had this problem until I met you."

"Neither did I," Janna said, feeling sensual heat rush through her as she arched her body against him in a long, intimate caress.

"So which one of us is going to be sensible about it?" he asked.

"How do you define sensible?"

"Not making love on a public beach," Raven said succinctly.

"Oh." Janna sighed. "Damn."

"Yeah. *Damn.*" With a reluctance that almost undid his good intentions, Raven slid his hand out from beneath Janna's sweater—but not before he saw the ruby nipple rising between his fingers. "Why am I always covering you up when all I want to do is run my tongue over you?" he groaned, easing the sweater back into place on her body.

Janna laughed softly. "Covering me up? Since when?"

"Since the first time I saw that ripe berry peeking out from beneath a corner of the survival blanket, that's when," he retorted. "All I wanted to do was take you into my mouth and feel you change as my tongue loved you."

Suddenly Janna remembered the moment when Raven had tucked the blanket around her shoulders and she had been devastated, thinking that he was utterly indifferent to her as a woman.

"You wanted me then?" she whispered, hardly able to believe it.

"I wanted you the instant I saw you fighting the storm," he said flatly.

"You should have taken me, Raven. I was yours the first time I heard your voice calling to me over the waves, telling me that I wasn't alone. I was yours before

I even knew who you were," she whispered. "I still am
yours. I always will be. I love—"

Janna felt the heat and sweetness of Raven's mouth
as he kissed her, stilling the torrent of whispered words.
It was a long time before he released her, laced his
fingers through hers and led her farther down the untouched sands. For an instant Janna closed her eyes,
walking blindly, trying to ease the pain of not being
allowed to speak her love. The wind combed through
her hair, freeing it from restraints, making it a soft
cinnamon radiance around her face.

The doubts that faded each time Raven made love to
Janna came back to her now with redoubled force. He was
an honest man, a compassionate man, a kind man. If he
didn't love her, he would try very hard not to hurt her. And
one of his kindnesses would be to make certain that she
wasn't left to hear her soft declarations of love echo unan-
swered. That was why he always kissed her words away,
sparing her all that he could. He had proven to her that
she was an endless fire in his body, but somehow she had
left his soul untouched. Passion, not love.

*Why can't one person love enough for two?*

No answer came to Janna's silent cry, nothing but the
wind keening over the unmarked sands.

Raven tried to look at the empty land and the wind-
tossed sea but could not glance away from Janna for
more than a few moments at a time. He sensed the
sadness in her, a darkness that only made her smile
more luminous, more achingly beautiful each time she
turned toward him. It was her courage that had drawn
him to Janna, even before he had seen her beauty and
sensuality. He sensed that courage now, a determination
to smile that was as great as her sadness. He ached to
hold her but knew that in the end it would only make

things worse for her, not better. Today he had to open his hands and return his gift from the gods.

"You're walking like a man with a destination," Janna said, holding her voice so tightly that her throat ached.

"Am I?"

"Yes. All broad shoulders and long-striding purpose."

Raven smiled at the image. "I just wanted to get up the beach before the illusions fade."

Janna gave him a sideways, here-we-go-again kind of look.

"A little farther, where the beach curves away to the north," he explained. "That's where they dance, but only on clear days."

There was a three-beat pause before Janna said triumphantly, "Bandersnatches, right? And it's 'wabes' not 'days.'"

"No, it's rose-colored mirages dancing between Eden and Alaska," he countered, stopping suddenly. "See?"

Janna felt the warmth of Raven radiating through her as he fitted her spine against his muscular chest. His powerful arm came over her shoulder as he pointed toward the northern horizon.

"There," he murmured. "See them dance?"

"Oh sure," she said agreeably. "Right next to the pink elephants tripping the light fantastic. They—" Janna's breath came in sharply and the hair on her neck stirred. Her eyes narrowed as she focused on the rose-tinted distance. *"Raven, there's something out there."*

"Yes," he whispered. "Aren't they beautiful? Everything man has ever wanted shimmering and dancing just beyond his reach."

Janna couldn't answer. The eerie, compelling illusions twisted and changed like pale rose flames, whispering to her soundlessly, haunting her. The rational, educated part of her mind calmly told her that the gently seething apparitions were simply a trick of light and atmosphere, like the mirages that had led so many desert explorers to madness and death; but the most primitive part of Janna looked at the illusions and saw pieces of her own soul calling soundlessly to her, telling her that everything she had ever dreamed of beckoned just beyond her fingertips.

The visions were drawn in flames of transparent silver and luminous rose, a world both dreamed and real. It was the sea and a deserted inlet and a single tree that was unique upon the face of the earth. It was a raven's song sung in silence and answered in the beauty of a smile. It was a man and a woman created for this radiant instant that knew no time, created for this beautiful and savage Eden, created each for the other. They glimmered and intertwined between sky and sea, time and timelessness, being and dreaming.

Raven saw Janna's face both haunted and radiant, sadness and ecstasy combined. He wanted to ask her what she was seeing in the enigmatic sky but knew that he had no right. Visions could only be shared, not demanded, a gift from one mind to another, one soul to another. He had taken too much from her already, more than he had any right to take. And he would pay for it in the torment of his memories when he touched again each moment of his days in Eden and thereby measured the immensity of his loss when he lived in Eden no longer.

Raven looked at the heartless, haunting mirages shimmering over the water; and he saw a time years ago, when he had been alone.

"The summer I built the cabin in Totem Inlet," Raven said quietly, "I was restless, lonely, a bird without wings, a fish without fins, nothing fit and nothing was right. I had been alone before, but never lonely." He hesitated, seeing again the summer that had begun so like this one and had ended so differently. "A few days after I finished the cabin I was restless again. I prowled through the forest, trying to wear myself out enough to sleep at night."

For an instant Raven closed his eyes, remembering, seeing a green Eden that at the time had looked more like hell.

"I found a young doe trapped in a moss-covered deadfall. She was half dead from thirst and terror and pain. When I freed her, I saw that one of her legs was injured. If I let her go, she would die. Yet if I kept her, tamed her, made her dependent on me, then I would be dooming her to a different, even more cruel death when I abandoned her. Because I knew the summer would end, the winter would come and I would go. I knew this, but the doe did not. She only knew each moment as it came."

Janna waited, feeling silence gathering like cold mist around her, chilling her. She sensed that she didn't want to know the end of the story Raven was telling.

And she had no choice but to know it, to understand the man she loved no matter what the cost.

"What did you do?" she whispered, forcing the words past the ache in her throat.

"I carried the doe to the cabin, bound her leg and wove cedar boughs into a fence upwind of the cabin. There was natural food, clean water and no bears to feed on her helplessness." Raven paused, seeing again the fragile, shivering doe who had calmed so quickly beneath his voice and hands. "It would have been very easy to win her trust. She was gentle, intelligent, adaptable as all young things are. She would have learned to run toward my voice, making me smile. She would have been company, and I was…lonely."

Janna started to ask why Raven had been so lonely, but he was talking again.

"I left the doe alone behind the cedar fence. When I checked on her I made sure that she neither saw nor scented me. In time she didn't limp anymore. She even chewed off the shirt I had used to bind her wound. The fence was high enough to restrain an injured doe, but not too high for a healthy one to jump. One day I came to check on her and found nothing there but silence and cedar."

Wind breathed across Janna's cheeks, cooling the tears that welled in her eyes. Raven saw the silver gleam and smoothed his palm very gently over Janna's hair.

"There was nothing sad in her leaving," he said. "My reward for helping the doe didn't come from winning her trust. My reward came when I saw her last graceful leap as she fled into the forest where she had been born. She never looked back. She never returned to the clearing or the cabin." Raven lifted his hand from Janna's hair. "And that was the way it had to be. To have taken anything more from the doe in her helplessness would have made me less of a man."

Janna bowed her head as she fought against tears and the realization that in some way Raven thought of her as he had the doe—something wounded, helpless, given into his care only long enough to be rescued, healed and then freed.

Like Angel. She had been another gift to be healed and freed. That was what Raven had meant when he said that he had finally realized Angel's life was more valuable than his chance to win her love. He had gone to her, pulled her out of the trap of her rage and despair, shown her the way to heal herself…and then watched her slip from his hands without a backward look.

At least Angel had finally returned. But did that make it better for Raven, or worse?

"It was Angel, wasn't it?" Janna whispered. "That's why you were restless the summer you built the cabin."

The slight trembling of Janna's voice made Raven wish that he had never brought her to this beach, this instant, tearing her illusions from her and leaving her nothing in their place. Yet illusions could be very cruel. Then they had to be taken away. Janna had to realize that she was free, that she owed nothing to the man who had pulled her from the sea, certainly not the love that she thought she felt.

"I don't feel that way now," Raven said quietly. "Seeing Angel and Hawk together brings me a feeling very close to joy."

"Now. But not then. Not the summer you built the cabin."

The slight flinching of Raven's eyelids told Janna that she was right.

"Angel had just married Hawk," Raven said, his voice rough with restraint. "I loved both of them, but seeing them together sometimes made me feel…" He hesitated.

"Terribly lonely," Janna whispered.

"It was nothing they did deliberately. It was just…" Again Raven paused, searching for words to describe the feelings he had never before tried to articulate.

"Seeing them made you wonder if you would ever love and be loved like that," Janna said.

Raven closed his eyes and wondered how Janna saw so easily, so clearly, into his soul. "Yes," he said simply.

"I love you like that, Raven."

"Hush, small warrior," he whispered, brushing the back of his fingers across Janna's cheek.

"Why?" Janna asked, her voice trembling. "Why won't you let me say that I love you?"

Raven breathed Janna's name against her hair as his hands closed around her shoulders with a force that he could barely control. He didn't let her turn toward him. He was afraid that if he saw her eyes he would be lost again, he would close his hands and keep her for himself because he had never felt so alive as he had when he was with her.

"What you feel is gratitude and passion, not love," Raven said, his voice so tightly held that it rasped harshly on his own ears. "You would have felt those things for any man who saved your life and then lacked the self-control and common decency to keep from seducing you while you were so vulnerable."

The bitterness and self-recrimination in Raven's voice shocked Janna. "That's not—" she began.

"No," Raven interrupted roughly. "Listen to me, Janna. You are a beautiful, incredibly sexy woman who married one of the few men around who couldn't appreciate you. I'll never forget our time together in Eden. I'll remember your wit and your laughter and your sensuality until I die."

*And the last word I say will be your name.*

Raven had just enough control left not to speak that cruel truth aloud. He had come to stand here on the shore of illusions and give back his gift from the gods. He had come here to release Janna, not to continue her captivity to the mistaken belief that she loved him.

"You owe me nothing," Raven continued, giving Janna no chance to speak. "We met by accident in a place out of time. There were no other people, nothing to remind you of your real life. You gave yourself to me out of gratitude, because I had taken you from the sea and you knew how violently I wanted you. If we had met any other way, you wouldn't have wanted me as a lover."

"That's not true," Janna whispered, trying to turn toward Raven but unable to move for the strength of his hands forcing her to face away from him. "I would have loved you if we'd met in Pike Place Market with a thousand people milling around and nothing more urgent on my mind than dinner. Haven't you been listening to me? I've always loved you, Raven. Always. That won't change—ever, anywhere, under any circumstances!"

"Janna," he said, wanting to believe her, knowing that he could not allow himself to reach for what he wanted so much that he couldn't trust himself anymore. Gratitude faded. Passion faded. Love endured. He knew that he wouldn't be able to let Janna go a few years or a few months from now. Or even a few hours. It had to be now. It had to be before she woke up in his arms and realized the difference between gratitude and love, before she looked at him with compassion and unhappiness. "Once you're back home, you'll think about what happened here. You'll see it differently. It will be like a dream. A joyous dream," he whispered very softly. "Please, God, at least that."

"What can I say to make you believe me?" Janna asked in despair. "Nothing can change how we met. Nothing can change how I feel about you now." She spun toward Raven suddenly, eluding his grasp, not caring that he would see the tears on her face. "Raven," she said, her voice trembling. "Raven, let me love you. Let yourself love me just a little in return. Raven, *please.*"

"Don't," he said gently, covering Janna's mouth with his hand. "I already hate myself for making love to you. Don't make it any worse."

Pain twisted through Janna, making her helpless. The realization that Raven regretted making love to her was devastating, taking the world out from beneath her feet, leaving her with nothing to hang on to but herself. Distantly she heard voices on the wind and thought that the rosy illusions were calling to her again, taunting her with the specter of things that would never be.

The voices dissolved into laughter. Angel and Hawk were coming up the beach, following the footprints of the two who had gone before. Angel, the woman Raven had once loved and lost and then finally loved again, but differently. Hawk, the man Angel loved in ways that she hadn't been able to love Raven. Raven had not only accepted that, he celebrated it, loving both Angel and Hawk equally, enjoying the visible evidence of their love for one another. Janna had learned to enjoy it, too. In the past few days she had come to appreciate the intelligence and courage that existed beneath Angel's honey-blond exterior. It was the same for Hawk, a gift for gentleness and laughter unexpected in a man of his hard good looks.

Yet suddenly Janna knew that she couldn't bear seeing Angel and Hawk together, much less take pleasure from their nearly tangible love. Not now. Not when she had just been told that the man she loved regretted ever having touched her.

She closed her eyes for an instant, gathering her courage. She had promised herself a perfect day before she spoke of love and it either was returned or not. She had had the day, she had spoken of love…and she had heard the gate to Eden closing behind her, leaving her alone in a world without love. All that remained was to walk away before she embarrassed Raven any further with her pleas.

"Are there really illusions out here?" Angel asked, coming up behind Raven.

"Delusions, actually," Janna said, her tone desperately normal as she opened her eyes. "There's a difference, you know. Like the difference between gimble and gambol, wabe and wave."

Angel went very still, sensing the pain in Janna even before she saw the evidence of spent tears. She looked at Raven. His face was hard, closed, as though he had been created from stone instead of flesh.

"Raven will explain it to you," Janna continued, looking through Angel. "He's good at inexplicable explanations. If you want to hear a real jaw-dropper, ask him about the difference between gratitude and love. Educational, I can assure you. A regular dissertation on sneezing bandersnatches."

"Janna," Raven said quietly. "You're not making any sense."

"Of course not. I left my brains at the bottom of an inlet." She looked around at the broad beach and the savage perfection of the land. "A pity this is Eden instead of the Ark. Two was a magic number for Noah and getting across water was no problem. But this is Eden and I have a ferry to catch. I'll bet the captain's name is Charon."

Without another word Janna turned and began walking away from the others, going where no tracks marred the glistening surface of the sand.

"Where are you going?" Raven asked.

"Across the river Styx."

"It ran around hell, not Eden."

"Somehow that doesn't surprise me."

"It's three miles to your cabin," Raven called. "Let Hawk take you home."

"It's all right, Raven," Janna said calmly, looking over her shoulder. "I'll walk on the edge of the sea. When the tide turns, it will be like I never was."

Raven closed his eyes, wanting to go to Janna, hold her, comfort her and himself. But it would be a cruelty, not a kindness. He had to be strong enough to be kind.

Janna watched Raven for a long moment before she turned away. She walked swiftly, cleanly, and she didn't look back again.

Raven opened his eyes and watched her until he could stand it no longer. Then he closed his eyes against the agony twisting through his soul.

"Carlson?"

Raven flinched from the soft voice and softer touch on his arm. Deliberately he stepped aside, beyond Angel's reach.

"Aren't you going to go after her?" Hawk asked.

"I never should have touched her." Raven's eyes opened. They were black, wild, almost frightening in their intensity. "I couldn't stop myself. I knew Janna was mine in some primitive, unspeakable way the first time I saw her. I *knew* it."

"So did she," Hawk said. "She loves you, Carlson. It shows in every—"

"Gratitude," Raven interrupted in a harsh tone. "Not love."

"How can you be so sure?" Angel asked.

His sudden laughter was as dark and savage as his eyes. "Angel Eyes," he said gently. "Sweet, beautiful Angel Eyes. It's so simple. I'm not the kind of man a woman loves. Of all people on earth, you should know that."

Angel went pale. "Carlson," she said, throwing her arms around him, "I never meant to hurt you like that. It was my fault, not yours. There's nothing wrong with you!"

"Don't cry for me," Raven said quietly, stroking the burnished gold of Angel's hair. "Even if I could, I wouldn't change what happened in the past. I'm not the other half of your soul, and I never could have been. Hawk is. And," Raven murmured, "you aren't the other half of mine. I know that now."

"But Janna is," Angel said urgently. "She's the other half of you."

"I know," Raven said. "And I know that gratitude isn't love."

"You're wrong about Janna," Hawk said quietly. "I was raised on gratitude, not love. I know what gratitude is and what it isn't. It isn't a woman's eyes following you everywhere, her fingers touching you when there's no need, her voice softening when she says your name, her smile more beautiful for you than for anyone else on earth."

Raven couldn't bear to hear any more words. He wanted to believe them too much. He no longer trusted himself to listen.

Abruptly he turned away and walked toward his car, letting his tracks mingle with the others, blurring all distinctions as to whom had gone out to the beach of illusions and who had returned. Yet still Hawk's voice followed, carrying clearly on the wind.

"Janna looks at you the way Angel looks at me. The way I look at Angel. The way you look at Janna. Not gratitude, Carlson. *Love!*"

Overhead, gulls wheeled on a gust of wind, keening

and crying to one another, and their calls became
Janna's name echoing in Raven's mind. The breakers
took up the cry, chanting in deeper tones, while the
wind's supple voice mourned in counterpoint. He saw
Janna wherever he looked, tasted her on his lips, felt her
in the heat of his own blood sliding through his veins.
She was everywhere, a part of everything; but most of
all she was part of his soul and he was crying her name
within the silence that only she had ever touched.

Raven drove quickly to the *Black Star*, wanting only
to pack up and get as far away from the Queen Charlotte Islands as possible. Once aboard he began stripping his clothes from lockers and drawers, throwing
things haphazardly into a duffel bag. He opened the last
drawer and froze. Angel's sketchbook lay on top, the
sketchbook that Janna had used in Totem Inlet.

Slowly Raven pulled the book out. He had never
looked at Janna's sketches. She had never offered to show
them to him, saying that after seeing Angel's stained glass
creations, anything else would be a disappointment.

The sketches were like Janna herself—direct, often
humorous, honest, and with an underlying sensuality of
line and shading that made Raven ache with memories.
He could hear her rueful laughter in the drawing labeled
"God's Own Washing Machine," which showed jeans
and shirts slung over any handy railing while rain poured
down over them, washing away salt and sand. He could
see Janna's honesty in the sketch of a totem labeled simply
"Before." She drew the Haida icons without embellish-
ment or softening, accepting without evasion the Haidas'
comfortless view of man in relation to the universe.

Page after page turned beneath Raven's careful
fingers until there was only one page left. He turned it
and felt his scalp tighten in primitive response. At first

the sketch looked like the others, but there were aspects of it that teased his mind until realization came. There were shadows that suggested a man's watchful eyes, a seemingly random collection of curves that became a face superimposed on the sea, a mist-wrapped mountain that evoked a man seated, thinking, a very powerful man with black hair and granite strength and eyes that flinched from nothing.

And all of the men were Raven.

Raven's features in infinite variations, his eyes and mouth repeated in forest and mountain, ocean and totem, Raven smiling or intent, asleep or in the grip of passion, calm or at the instant of hottest ecstasy, gentle or fierce—Raven, always Raven. It was as though nothing lived, not even the sea itself, that wasn't animated by Raven's own breath, his own life flowing into everything, becoming part of it.

He looked at the drawing until he could no longer see it, and then he put his face in his hands and wept, knowing that he had finally heard a love song for a raven.

Mist condensed with the falling sun, giving the land a mysterious gloaming that was as haunted as the vanished rose illusions. Janna had stopped a hundred yards from her cabin and turned to look at the long, wandering trail she had left on her walk out of Eden. She didn't know how long she had been standing there watching the ragged black stitches she had left behind in the sand, stitches that were being unraveled by the returning tide. Now there was nothing left but shadowy hollows where spindrift gathered. The next wave would wash away even that, leaving nothing at all.

"If I could, I would paint sky and mountains, sea and forest, and they would all be you."

The soft, deep voice sent shivers over Janna's skin and made her doubt her sanity in the instant before she spun around. Raven was standing within reach, as though he had condensed from the primal night and her own dreams.

"If I could," Raven said, "I would have the wind calling your name in all times and seasons, and the mist-veiled forests would have been created just to match your eyes. But I'm not an artist or a god. I'm only a harsh-voiced raven flying over an empty Eden, crying for what I wanted so much that I was afraid to believe that it was finally mine." His big hands came up, framing Janna's face, trembling as they touched her softness and warmth. "I have no beautiful songs to fill your silences, no worlds to remake in your image, no special way to tell you that you're the other half of my soul."

"Raven—" Janna's voice broke. "I don't need special gifts or songs or anything but you. Just you, Raven. *I love you.*"

The words swept through Raven, transforming him.

He lifted her high in his arms and held her close, telling her with his strength and his gentleness and his whispered words how much he loved her, feeling his love returned with every touch, every breath, her vital warmth enveloping him as he held her.

Beyond them the last of the footprints leading from Eden dissolved into the mist and moon-silvered sea. Neither Janna nor Raven noticed. They had found the only Eden that mattered, and they would hold it forever in their arms.

*Everything you love about romance...*
***and more!***

*Please turn the page for Signature Select™*
*Bonus Features.*

# Love Song
## FOR A RAVEN

BONUS
FEATURES
INSIDE

# TOP TEN

Summer Love Stories

by Hilda Rasula

Maybe it's the fresh air. Or the skin-revealing warm-weather fashions. Accountability aside, it's a timeless truth that the rapidly rising mercury often overheats more than just your car's engine. Combine fresh experiences away from home with the introduction of a new acquaintance and you have two potent ingredients for the kindling of romance and adventure. Not to be missed, the ten movies below are ageless coming-of-age stories that incorporate the topic we thrill to remember: summer lovin'.

## 1. *Dirty Dancing* (1987)

*Starring Jennifer Grey, Patrick Swayze*

In the summer of 1963 a young idealist, "Baby," travels with her family to a resort in New York's Catskills. There she meets Johnny Castle, a dance instructor from the wrong side of the tracks. When Baby has to learn the mambo to fill in for Johnny's dance partner, she also receives some lessons in love and life, as she and Johnny start an affair that opens their eyes to a new world of possibilities. Dynamite dancing and a great soundtrack are sure to please in this red-hot romance.

## 2. *Say Anything* (1989)
*Starring John Cusack, Ione Skye, John Mahoney, Lili Taylor*
John Cusack is unforgettable as Lloyd Dobler, a lovable loner whose interests include kickboxing, not finding a career and Diane (Skye), the beautiful class brain. Socially, Lloyd and Diane are worlds apart, but during the summer following graduation, they become closer than either of them could have ever predicted. This quirky, endearing film takes a refreshingly honest look at teen love, and also offers some of the most romantic moments ever seen on the big screen. Peter Gabriel's romantic song "In Your Eyes" is featured in the film.

## 3. *The Bridges of Madison County* (1995)
*Starring Clint Eastwood, Meryl Streep*
In Iowa farm country in the summer of 1965, Robert Kincaid, a seasoned photographer, knocks on the door of housewife Francesca Johnson. Francesca, whose husband and children are away at the state fair, is an underappreciated Italian-American whose isolated life has left certain

dreams unfulfilled. She agrees to give Robert a tour of the covered bridges in the area that he plans to shoot for *National Geographic*. He stays with her for four days, and what unfolds is a love so intimate, so true, that it becomes the highlight of their lives. Beautifully directed by Eastwood, and with superb acting, this achingly tender film is a must-see for romance fans!

## 4. *Mystic Pizza* (1988)
*Starring Julia Roberts, Annabeth Gish, Lili Taylor, Vincent D'Onofrio*

This heartfelt chick flick is a great choice to watch with friends. It centers around three young working-class women and their adventures and struggles with first love in small-town Mystic, Connecticut, during one fateful summer. Daisy (Roberts), flirtatious and beautiful, sets her sights on a rich preppy; Kat (Gish), cautious and sensitive, is about to enter the Ivy League world, but falls for an older married man; and Jojo (Taylor) loves her fiancé and loves sex...but gets faint at the thought of tying the knot. Watch this stirring coming-of-age movie for its empathetic characters and excellent performances.

## 5. *Before Sunrise* (1995)
*Starring Ethan Hawke, Julie Delpy*

When American traveler Jesse meets French student Celine on the Eurail train and the two share a moment of connection, he asks her to stop in Vienna with him for a one-night date. Over the course of fourteen hours spent getting to know each other, Jesse and Celine transcend what they know is the cliché of their situation, and experience what it is to truly be with another person and love them. Part whimsy, part profound philosophy, *Before Sunrise* is a special romance, highlighted by great performances and the beautiful sights of Vienna.

## 6. *Grease* (1978)
*Starring John Travolta, Olivia Newton-John*
This beloved musical about 1950s nostalgia starts with the "summer lovin'" of "greaser" Danny and girl-next-door Sandy. When they find themselves attending the same high school for senior year, they struggle to reconcile their different social worlds. Love wins out in the end, of course, after much hilarious sexual tension and fantastic singing and dancing.

## 7. *Paradise* (1991)
*Starring Melanie Griffith, Don Johnson, Elijah Wood, Thora Birch*
At the heart of this delicate drama is Willard (Wood), a ten-year-old boy who is sent to live with his pregnant mother's friends for the summer. Ben

and Lily Reed, a couple that once was happy, now live together like strangers, torn apart by tragedy. When Willard enters their lives, subtle shifts occur—for the Reeds, for Willard himself and for the impish girl next door who becomes Willard's best friend. Lovingly crafted with fine detail, and with the beautiful countryside of South Carolina as the backdrop, this heartfelt film is part coming-of-age story, part love story...and all charm.

## 8. *The Man in the Moon* (1991)
*Starring Reese Witherspoon, Jason London, Sam Waterston, Tess Harper*

Fourteen-year-old Dani (Witherspoon) is a precocious tomboy who starts the rocky road to womanhood in rural Louisiana in the summer of 1957. Dani admires her pretty older sister Maureen, and wonders if she will ever be as popular with boys, until one day her abstract fantasies materialize in the form of Court (London), a seventeen-year-old boy who moves nearby. Unfortunately for Dani, Court prefers Maureen.... A nostalgic and perfect exploration of adolescence and first love, this exquisite heartbreaker features a riveting young Reese Witherspoon.

## 9. *Slums of Beverly Hills* (1998)
*Starring Natasha Lyonne, Marisa Tomei, Alan Arkin*

Your brothers are jerks, your dad gambles so much that you have to keep moving to avoid paying rent and your mother, who divorced him, lives on the other side of the country. This would be bad enough, but for fourteen-year-old Vivian, things get terribly worse when she blossoms into womanhood (and a large, attention-getting cup size) seemingly overnight. In this heartfelt comedy, set in the summer in the early 1970s, one girl struggles with the painful embarrassments of adolescence, including the awkwardness and intrigue of her first love interest.

## 10. *Rambling Rose* (1991)

*Starring Laura Dern, Robert Duvall, Diane Ladd, Lukas Haas*

In 1930s Georgia, Rose, a sweet but irrepressibly sexed-up girl, enters the lives of a liberal-minded family. They've taken her in to help her escape a compromised past, but her sensuality seems to get in the way of all her relations with men, including the family patriarch and his intensely curious teenage son. This tale is steeped in Southern atmosphere and poignancy, mostly thanks to a sensitive, intelligent script and outstanding acting. Rent this one for a sultry summer night.

Note: Originally published online at www.eHarlequin.com

# Summer Flings: Explore Romance in the Great Outdoors

by Olga Tirsalis

The summer sun may be sweltering, but that's no excuse not to generate some heat of your own. Indulge in the sizzle of a summer fling: whether you've been together a week, a month, or years,
10 your relationship deserves—in fact, *requires*—some passionate escapades only the warm weather can induce. So get out there and experience romance in the great outdoors.

Stumped for ideas? No worries: we've got a selection of sinful summer trysts for the choosing....

**Earth & Water**
Heat, humidity, blazing sun—the makings of a truly "hot" romance. Okay, we admit blistering heat-wave weather may not be conducive to *movement,* let alone to sparking a passionate embroilment. But what better time to turn on the backyard sprinkler, don a sexy T-shirt and engage in a water balloon fight à deux? If you're really

feeling frisky, pile on the dirt and have a mud bath—or brawl! Go ahead, get soiled and silly!

### Child's Play

Who says flying a kite is for kids? Nonsense! Go to your local park, string 'er up and chase the wind. Follow the kite—skip, run, walk—and enjoy the carefree spirit this floating object inspires.

### Think Outside the Box...

And get a tent! Go camping, build a makeshift fire and roast some marshmallows. Who knows? You may just kindle more than a few flames yourselves. And, as you know those summer nights can get awfully chilly, so use it as an excuse to snuggle up in a sleeping bag for one!

### Get Your Motor Running

Ah, the open road—there's nothing like it! The wind whipping through your hair, the sun on your back, the tight embrace as you ride, the feeling of utter freedom with no planned itinerary in mind. Just get up, get on and go!

### Frolic in the Foliage

Is the grass greener on the other side? Why not find out together? Take a walk, barefoot, and let the blades brush against your skin. Indulge in the cold, sometimes sharp but smooth texture. Pack a picnic lunch to fully appreciate the greenery.

**More than Just Movies**
The theater may require you to leave the house, but it's still an indoor event—interesting, though it may be. Instead, why not take in a carnival or outdoor music festival? Play some games, listen to some tunes and get some sun while you're at it. What better way to enjoy the season?

**Sandy Sensations**
Water. Beads of sweat. Glistening bodies. Just as good ol' Mother Nature intended! That's right, a day at the beach. It's an outdoor attraction that's hard to top: what with the lotions, the water sports and the sand castles, the possibilities are endless.

12 **Set Adrift on Bliss**
Not too keen on camping gear and hiking? Too much effort involved? Then slip into a hammock and gently sway in the sun. Not only will this soothe your soul after a long day, but it can also jump-start those fantastic dreams....

**Animal Magnetism**
Bet you never thought the zoo or neighborhood petting farm could solicit such prowess in your amour. Well, it's true—exploring wildlife together can trigger pheromones you never even knew existed! The thrill of the hunt awaits you...

**They Don't Call It "Great" for Nothing!**
We're always huddled inside. Even when we prepare for a romantic encounter, it usually

consists of dinner, drinks, perhaps a show—but all indoors. Most venues cater to the inwardly inclined. Well, this may be suitable for those blah winter months, but why not enjoy the great outdoors and all it has to offer in the summertime?

Experience Mother Nature in all her splendor, and with minimal effort. Infuse your brain with the sights, smells and textures only she can conjure. How to intensify this sensory seduction? Simply, get out there—*anywhere*—outside, and just enjoy the warm weather. No need for an itemized schedule, just see where the day takes you.

Note: Originally published online at www.eHarlequin.com

# A PERFECT MATCH
## by Emilie Rose

## CHAPTER ONE

No man should be forced to endure a baby shower.

Tate Sumner fingered the irregularly shaped piece of cardboard in his pocket. He'd been ordered to mingle until he found the guest whose puzzle piece linked with his, and then they were supposed to mimic with their bodies the way the pieces fit together. Leave it to his matchmaking sister, Sandy, to turn her baby shower, traditionally a females-only affair, into a dating service. Ha, ha. Hilarious. Not. At thirty-four, he sometimes felt out of sync—too young for marriage and all it entailed, but too old for singles' games.

In the past hour he'd worked his way through the crowd without a match and without enthusiasm, although he had to admit, there'd been a few amusing tussles as the mostly single, twentysomething guests linked up. No doubt the free-flowing alcoholic beverages had loosened their inhibitions.

He didn't overindulge anymore. The hell-raising and skirt-chasing days he'd once enjoyed had come to an abrupt end after a building collapse landed him in the hospital last year, making him realize how short life was. Before that life-changing event, he'd have let one of the blond twins beside him convince him to go home with her tonight. He subtly checked his watch and then shot another glance at the front door. No offense to Tia or Leah, but he'd rather catch the second half of the Braves game.

The doorbell rang. His sister unearthed herself from a pile of torn pastel wrapping paper and waddled to answer as fast as her due-any-day-now pregnant belly would allow. And then she screamed and launched herself at the poor victim on her welcome mat. With his luck the newcomer would be his match, and he'd be making a human puzzle piece out of himself soon. Not an anticipated event.

His sister dragged the visitor into view, and Tate nearly dropped the glass of spiked lemonade someone had forced into his hand. *Faith King.* He hadn't seen her since his youngest sister, Sandy, had married Faith's brother, David, two years ago. Faith's strawberry-blond hair hung in a smooth, glossy curtain curling just below her jawline. He missed the tangles he'd created during their passionate night after the rehearsal dinner.

Desire kicked him in the gut. They'd torched the sheets that night, so he hadn't understood the deep freeze Faith had treated him to the next day at the wedding and reception. Sure, he'd expected a little morning-after awkwardness since they'd fallen into bed without the usual get-to-know-you dance, but he'd hoped they'd fill in the gaps during the remainder of the weekend. It hadn't happened. Faith had avoided him as if he'd exposed her to something contagious.

And then, in a fit of wounded pride, he'd had a pint too much champagne at the reception, danced with every female present and shot off his mouth with a lousy toast. Yeah, he'd been a real prize. A prize idiot.

"I'm sorry I'm late." Faith dragged her rolling suitcase over the threshold. "The storm delayed my flight. I didn't even stop by the hotel. I had the taxi bring me straight here."

Her slightly husky and somewhat breathless voice sucked Tate right back to their middle-of-the-night tussles. They'd christened his sofa, his bed and even his kitchen counter. For years he'd craved the carefree bachelor life he'd been denied while helping to raise his younger sisters, but in the days preceding Sandy's wedding, Faith had made him want more than one wild weekend. She'd tempted him to forget the promise he'd made to himself to savor the freedom that came with getting his last sister out of the house and *finally* being responsible for only himself.

"You have men at your baby shower." Faith scanned the gathering with a frown, and then she spotted him and his wannabe companions. His heart kicked irregularly as her shock-widened blue eyes inspected him from cowlick to boots.

Her lush lips compressed, and her gaze hit his with the same arctic blast he remembered from their final encounter. After seeing off the bride and groom that day, he'd asked Faith for her number. She'd slammed the car door in his face. Her glare tonight indicated they wouldn't be sharing a fond reunion. The knowledge slid down his spine like a hot cinder.

His sister, Sandy, wiggled her fingers, motioning Tate forward. He excused himself from the twins and joined his sister. "You remember David's sister, Faith, don't you?"

Oh, yeah. Every luscious curve of her. He had no trouble recalling Faith's scent, the silkiness of her skin, her gasps of passion or the hot, wet clench of her body.

"She wanted to be here for her niece's arrival." Sandy's words dragged him back to the present.

He locked gazes with the woman who starred in his dreams far too often. "Faith."

"Tate." Her tone could give a man frostbite, but the blush tinting her cheeks confirmed she hadn't forgotten what had happened between them, either.

"Faith is checking into the Hilltop Inn for a few days. Next week she's closing on a brand-new house here in Chapel Hill." Sandy nudged him. "Put her suitcase in my room for now, would you, Tate? And get her a drink, please."

His heart pumped harder. Faith would be living minutes away in town instead of eight hours away in Atlanta. He offered her his glass. "Here. Take mine. I haven't touched it, but watch out for the kick. My twisted sister enjoys watching her guests get sloshed while she stays sober."

Faith extended her hand. Their fingers brushed as she took the drink, and a current flowed from her fingers to his. Her eyes widened, but quickly filled with wariness.

"Thank you."

His sister took Faith's umbrella and propped it against the wall. "Do you have your puzzle piece?"

Faith blinked and averted her gaze. "Yes. It's in my purse."

"Dig it out, introduce yourself to everyone until you find your match. Tate can explain the rules of the game. I need to sit down." Sandy winced, pressed a hand to her lower back and waddled slowly back to her chair, leaving Tate with Faith in the foyer.

"How are you?" he asked. Faith looked incredible—still curvy in all the right places.

She dug in her leather purse and withdrew the puzzle piece. Tate rocked back on his heels. Interesting. It didn't take a fireman who spent too many hours of downtime at the station assembling puzzles to see that Faith's piece was counterpart to the one in his pocket. His impatience with the stupid party game evaporated, and his blood hummed in anticipation of fitting his body to hers.

Coincidence? Or was his sister matchmaking?

"I'm well. Good to see you again, Tate. Excuse me, I need to mingle with the other guests and find my match. Don't let me keep you from your friends." She delivered the words in a polite, but chilly, brush-off.

He produced his piece of the puzzle and aligned it with hers. "No need. I'm your man."

"Match!" shrieked Sandy from the living room, confirming Tate's matchmaking theory. God bless little sisters. He took back every negative thing he'd ever said about the baby of the family.

"Know what that means, Faith?" He took the tumbler out of her hand and set it on the credenza.

She shifted on her feet and bit her luscious bottom lip. "No."

"It means we get to simulate the interlocking puzzle pieces with our bodies." Damn, he couldn't wait. He barely restrained himself from rubbing his hands in glee.

Scowling, she looked at her piece. It had the jutting male projection, whereas his had the indented female shape. The pieces fit together perfectly—just as he and Faith had that night. A moment passed and then Faith lifted her hands to his shoulders. He cupped her waist, and his heart thumped in expectation of her tongue in his mouth, but then she swiftly lifted her knee toward his groin. He sucked in a swift breath and tensed in anticipation of pain.

She stopped just short of her target. "Need I continue?"

BONUS FEATURE

## CHAPTER TWO

FAITH KING WATCHED the gleam in Tate—the snake's—green eyes turn from seductive to cautious. She ignored the strength and heat of the thick shoulder muscles beneath her hands, lowered her knee and stepped out of reach before the urge to tangle her fingers in his short dark hair and seal her lips to his won out over common sense.

A muscle ticked in Tate's rock-hard jaw. "You've made your point."

Two years ago she'd been rapidly cartwheeling into love during her brother's prewedding festivities. Tate had been playing a game…or so Faith had learned when she arrived at the church to dress with the bride and the other bridesmaids. The women had been laughing about firefighter Tate's reputation for starting sensual fires all over town, and wagering on which wedding guest he'd go home with that night. No one had known Faith had just spent the most passionate night of her life in his bed.

In seconds, she'd gone from euphorically believing she'd finally found Mr. Right to the sinking realization that she'd been just another body to Tate Sumner.

Sandy had explained that Tate had wild oats to sow because he'd spent his teens and twenties acting as a father figure to his four younger siblings after their father died. If Faith had doubts about Tate's interest in a long-term relationship, his wedding toast had certainly clarified them.

"I don't know why any man under fifty would settle for just one woman, but good luck, pal, and by the way, I'll break your legs if you hurt my sister."

"You're moving to town." Tate's direct gaze pinned her in place and caused her pulse to quicken. She'd forgotten how good he smelled and how his brawny build made her feel delicate and protected. She hadn't forgotten the strength of his arms as he held her, but not for lack of trying on her part. Nor had she forgotten he was a charmer like her father.

"Yes. I wanted to be near David, Sandy and my soon-to-be-born niece. I've accepted a position as a physician's assistant at the hospital."

"How about dinner tomorrow night?"

She nearly choked. Did he think she'd fall back into his bed as easily as she had the first time? Never mind that Tate had the sexiest, greenest eyes she'd ever seen or strong, capable *and talented* hands. She was wise to his seductive ways and had no intention of being sucked in by his charming smile or clever words again. "No, thanks. I try not to repeat my mistakes."

He blinked, briefly covering his eyes with long, thick lashes any woman would envy, but his confident smile didn't waver. "Your loss, Faith. I remember how hot we were together even if you don't."

She hardened herself against the sexy rumble of his voice and tried to ignore the temptation nipping at her heels. "Perhaps your memory is faulty."

A wicked grin lifted one corner of his edible mouth and carved a crease in his cheek—a crease she'd traced with her tongue once upon a time. "Maybe you're afraid you can't live up to my memories."

24    Her molars clicked together. "And maybe you're overestimating your charms and those memories are not worth revisiting."

His grin faded. "I didn't hear you complaining. In fact, I could swear your screams of pleasure are what made my neighbor hammer on the apartment wall and ask us to keep it down. He didn't realize keeping *it* down around you was impossible."

Fire rushed through Faith's veins. She lifted her chin and pretended that incident hadn't been the most embarrassing, yet hilarious moment of her life. Tate had carried her from the kitchen back to the bedroom where they'd made love with silent laughter. She'd never had so much fun making love before. "It's amazing how far a woman will go to bolster a man's

ego. If I remember correctly you needed a little…
encouragement."

Tate's eyes darkened. "For crying out loud, we'd made love three times in as many hours. Did you expect me to go off like an adolescent each time? And I don't remember you complaining about the extra action." He grabbed her suitcase and marched with it toward the bedroom.

Faith fisted her hands and counted to ten. Was she an idiot? Why goad him? Certainly, his stamina had put her previous lovers to shame. And yes, she'd loved the fact that Tate had unselfishly delayed his pleasure until she'd found her own. And darn it, why couldn't she forget how good he'd made her feel in bed and out of it?

Swallow your pride and keep it friendly, Faith. Sandy worships her brother, and David is the only family you acknowledge. Exclude Tate and you could be excluded. "Tate, wait."

She followed him into Sandy and David's bedroom and then wished she hadn't. Standing beside Tate and a bed melted her like candle wax. He'd been an amazing lover. Probably because he'd had so much practice, she reminded herself bitterly. "My gift for the baby is in my suitcase."

His thick biceps bunched as he effortlessly lifted the case onto the bed as if it hadn't gone over the airline's weight limit, and then he stepped back to allow her access, but he didn't leave the room. She wished he had as soon as she unzipped and opened the case. Her lingerie lay on top, and her skin burned as she dug through the colorful bras and panties to reach the gift-wrapped package cushioned beneath them. She shoved a pair of pink panties—the ones he'd pulled off her *with his teeth* that night—to the bottom of the case.

"Where is the house you're buying?" he asked.

She closed the case before meeting his gaze. Clutching the gift to her chest she replied, "Rocky Creek."

"Nice neighborhood. My district. Station Six. Give me your address and I'll have the platoon look out for you when I'm off-duty."

Faith shifted her jaw and considered his words. "Are you being nice or are you just trying to get my address?"

"I could get your address from Sandy or David, but I'm asking you. You're family now."

*Family.* Everyone seemed to have their own definition of the word. Faith shoved back her hair and immediately recalled the gentle tangle of Tate's fingers in the strands. "Why can't you just accept that night was a mistake, and I'm not interested in a repeat?"

"Because when you lie you get a tiny red patch right here." He traced a blunt finger over the skin at the top of her breastbone just below her locket. Faith's breath hitched and her pulse leapt. Her brother had a big mouth. He must have told Tate about the telltale sign. That spot had been the bane of Faith's childhood. She'd never been able to get away with anything.

Tate's warm fingers curled around her nape, choking off coherent thought. He erased the distance between them. Heat radiated off his body, and his woodsy scent enclosed her in a seductive fog. "Are you going to deny you've thought about that night?"

Deny it. But she couldn't form the lie. Her mouth watered and her lips dried. What little resistance she had evaporated as his head lowered. Faith pressed her hands against his chest. His heart pounded beneath her palm, and his warm breath swept her lips a split second before his mouth took hers in a slow, lazy kiss. He sampled her mouth with lips, tongue and teeth until her knees buckled. One big hand stroked down her spine to cup her bottom and support her weight, forging her to his length.

*Wow.* She'd forgotten his potency and seriously overestimated her willpower. Her skin tingled and her belly tightened. She couldn't find the strength to shove him away and was on the verge of dragging him onto David's bed and making a fool out of herself again when her common sense rallied. Good grief. Get a grip. He's just like your father. She yanked free and moved out of reach. "Between playmates, Tate?"

Before he could reply, Sandy stumbled into the room looking nauseated. "Sorry, guys. I think I ate too much guacamole. I need to lie down. Tate, can you give Faith a ride to her hotel?"

Tate's jaw muscles flexed. His gaze drilled hers. "Be glad to."

## CHAPTER THREE

"WHAT DO YOU MEAN you've given up my room?" Faith sounded nearly hysterical.

Tate considered defusing the situation, but he was in the mood to chew nails right now and he'd probably make matters worse by intervening. How could Faith stubbornly deny the attraction between them? Hell, she'd melted in his arms with one kiss. He hadn't found that potent a chemistry before or since their night together—not because he hadn't looked.

"I'm sorry, Ms. King. It's graduation weekend for both of the local universities, and it's almost midnight. When you didn't arrive by 7:00 p.m. as expected we thought you weren't coming, and we released your room."

"Then give me another one."

"We're at full occupancy."

Faith made a noise of disgust. "Are you telling me there's no room at the inn?"

"Yes, ma'am."

"Find one," Tate barked.

The clerk startled. "Sir—"

Tate straightened to his full six feet four inches and glared. He didn't use his size to intimidate often, but once in a while it came in handy.

"I'll try. One moment, please." The clerk picked up the phone and made several calls in rapid succession while Faith paced in front of the marble counter—an action that gave Tate time to admire her legs beneath the just-above-knee-length skirt and to remember how good they'd felt wrapped around him. Ten minutes later the clerk nervously cleared his throat. "Ms. King, the only room I can find is at the Streetside Motel."

"I'll take it," Faith insisted.

"No way," Tate replied. "The place is unsafe, Faith. Streetside rents rooms by the hour."

Her eyebrows puckered and then rose. Wide-eyed, she stared at him. "You mean—?"

"Yeah. Hookers."

Her cheeks turned rosy. She studied her shoes. "Never mind. I'll borrow David's couch."

"You could always stay at my place. At least you know my bed's comfortable." He couldn't resist the dig. Not that they'd slept much that night. And he wouldn't sleep a wink knowing she was back between his sheets, alone, but he'd just begun his four-day-off rotation. He'd catch up on sleep tomorrow.

Her spine stiffened and her straight little nose lifted. "I don't think so."

"David's couch it is." He carried her bag back to his pickup truck, helped Faith into the vehicle and headed back where they'd come from. Five miles down the road his cell phone rang. "Sumner."

"Tate, it's David. Sandy's in labor. We're on the way to the hospital."

His stomach bottomed out. His baby sister. A mom. Jeez. Where had time gone? It seemed like only yesterday Tate had been stuck at home babysitting his sisters and resenting every minute of it while their mother worked nights and weekends to support them. After high school graduation he'd immediately gone into firefighter training instead of college as planned. His dad's life insurance payment was running out and they'd needed the income. Tate had believed life and fun were passing him by while he juggled the roles of Mr. Mom and man of the house. The building collapse last year had reminded him of what was really important. *Family.*

The sound of Sandy's moan through the phone made Tate feel helpless. As a firefighter-paramedic, he was trained to dash in and rescue people. He could even deliver a baby if the situation demanded it, but there were parts of his sister he'd rather not become acquainted with. "I'll relay the news to Faith and then Mom. David, your sister will be staying at my place tonight. The hotel screwed up her reservation."

BONUS FEATURE

Faith squeaked indignantly beside him. Tate sent his love to Sandy, finished his conversation with David and disconnected before turning to Faith. "Sandy's in labor and on the way to the hospital. I don't have a key to their town house. Do you?"

Faith pinched the bridge of her nose and scrunched her eyes closed. "No."

"Then you're bunking with me unless you have a better idea."

Her shoulders sagged. "No, no better idea. But I won't sleep with you. I'll take your couch."

His mother and sisters would have his hide if he put a female guest in the den. Too bad Mom now lived in Florida with his aunt, and Faith couldn't use Mom's guest room. "Not a chance. The sofa's mine— if you refuse to share my big ol' king-size bed."

"I do refuse. Besides, you sleep in the middle."

Grinning, he pulled his truck into his assigned parking space and killed the engine. "Only with you, Faith."

An expression of disbelief crossed her face. "Does that line usually work for you?"

He deserved her sarcasm. Two years ago, a good time was all he'd wanted, but bachelorhood wasn't as great as he'd imagined, and whether Faith knew it or not, she was the only woman with whom he'd ever spent an entire night. He usually said his goodbyes before the awkward morning after. He circled the truck and met her beside her door. "It's not a line."

She ignored the helping hand he offered. "You have a reputation for starting fires all over Chapel Hill, Tate. Don't try lighting one with me."

"Me? I'm a firefighter. I put out fires."

Her lips compressed. "Not with women."

Understanding clicked into place. His little sister always had yapped too much.

What had Sandy told her? "I'm thirty-four and single. Am I not allowed a personal life?"

"You might want to warn the women involved that you're only in it for the fun and games before you take them back to your black leather-and-chrome bachelor pad."

His heart missed a beat. "Were you wanting more than fun and games that night, Faith?"

She snorted. "In your dreams, hose jockey."

Hose jockey. Slang for the newest recruits. "I'm a captain now."

She waved a hand and shoved back her hair. "Whatever. It's late. I'm exhausted."

He was anything but tired. Adrenaline raced through his veins. He attributed his restlessness to Sandy's labor…and Faith's return. "Let's get you tucked in."

Ignoring her scowl, he hefted her case from the truck bed and led the way to his second-floor apartment. They'd both been a little tipsy from champagne and overheated from some heavy petting in his truck the last time he'd brought her here. She'd been twined around him like a kudzu vine, with her legs circling his waist and her tongue in his ear when he'd carried her from the parking lot straight to his bed. He'd been seconds away from detonation and the hottest sex of his life. Too bad tonight wouldn't be a repeat.

But there was always tomorrow.

## CHAPTER FOUR

FAITH RELUCTANTLY ENTERED Tate's apartment. Every-thing was uncomfortably familiar to her from their long-ago tryst—the sofa, even the kitchen held memories of the intense passion they'd shared…. Returning to the scene of the crime held no appeal for her. The crime? Tate had stolen Faith's heart two years ago and none of the frantic dating she'd done in the Atlanta singles scene since had repaired the damage.

How could you replace a man who seemed to anticipate your every thought, every need? But then, according to Sandy's bridesmaids, Tate had more ex-perience with women than a librarian had with books. Anticipating a woman's needs was probably second nature to him. Faith paused in the doorway of his bedroom. Her palms moistened and her blood raced. The kiss at David's hadn't helped the situation. She had to get through this weekend with her heart intact and her knees together.

"You remember where everything is?" Tate asked from just behind her. His gravelly voice slid down her spine like the drag of a callused fingertip. She shivered, cursed the warmth puddling in her belly and nodded. "Then help yourself to towels and whatever else you want."

She couldn't look at him. Instead, she studied the wide black leather headboard and the black comforter. She'd spent too much time pressed against the first and buried beneath the second—first in person and then later in her dreams. "Please wake me if David calls with news about Sandy and the baby."

"Sure, but it'll probably be hours. There are extra hangers in my closet, and here's an empty drawer if you want to unpack."

The intimacy of the situation made her uncomfortable. She'd never lived with a man. "Do you need to shower while I unpack?"

"That'd be great." He disappeared into the adjoining bathroom.

Faith struggled to block out the sound of running water and the image of his naked body beneath the spray, but her brain insisted on recalling his slick flesh in graphic detail. Her breathing turned shallow. They'd shared his shower that night. She'd been convinced he was Mr. Right. How could she have been so wrong? She shoved her underwear into the drawer. It wasn't like her to tumble into bed with any available male, but she'd been vulnerable before David's wedding. She'd lost her mother six months earlier, her thirtieth birthday had loomed and her friends had been marrying and producing children at an alarming rate. David was moving out. Faith had felt alone. The final straw had been her father's insensitive request days before David's wedding. He'd wanted to bring his girlfriend to the ceremony.

Faith sank onto the bed and put her head in her hands. She'd known her father was a liar and a cheat since she was twelve years old. Her parents argued often, and after each argument her father would beg forgiveness and swear not to stray again. Her mother had forgiven him every time, but Faith had seen the pain in her mother's eyes. Had the pain of betrayal weakened her mother to the disease that had taken her life?

Faith's head had been reeling when she'd met Tate. He'd seemed so family-centered and devoted to his siblings—the antithesis of Faith's selfish father. Had the shattering of her world made her susceptible to Tate's rugged charm and blinded her to his womanizing ways? A man who belonged on a hunky fireman's calendar probably had women throwing themselves at him regularly, and the blondes vying for his attention tonight at the baby shower proved he liked women *plural,* didn't it?

The bathroom door opened and Tate exited in a cloud of steam. Water droplets clung to his bare chest and broad shoulders and sparkled in his damp hair. The towel knotted at his waist revealed his long, strong legs. Her mouth dried and her blood simmered.

She wished the chemistry between them would evaporate along with the bathroom steam.

"Faith, are you okay?" He crossed the room and stopped in front of her.

She was a fool for wanting a man with so much charisma. Tate, like her father, was movie-star handsome. Also, like her father, he worked many hours away from home. Could she trust him? Rhetorical question. Tate wasn't looking for forever, just for now. "I'm just tired."

"Are you sure?" He knelt beside the bed and cupped a long-fingered hand over her knee. Heat raced upward from the point of contact. Was the concern in his eyes genuine? She didn't trust her judgment, but she seriously wished she could lean her head on his broad, damp shoulder. Had David told him about their father's repeated infidelities? She shook her head and rose, displacing his hand.

He stood beside her. "Call if you need anything… like someone to scrub your back." The teasing glint in his eyes made her stomach flip-flop. Where was her common sense?

"Good night, Tate." As soon as he left the room she rushed through her shower, trying to forget that just minutes before he'd been naked in the glass stall. She turned out the bedroom light and darkness swallowed her. She slid between the sheets and his scent enveloped her. Her pulse pounded. Faith closed her eyes and courted elusive sleep.

"FAITH." Tate's rough voice nudged her toward consciousness. She smelled coffee. Were they going to make love in the kitchen again? Last time she'd knocked over the canister and spilled coffee grounds all over the counter.

She nuzzled deeper into her pillow. "We can't. Not again. Your neighbor will hear us."

"Faith." His voice sounded harder, more insistent this time.

"Again? Are you insatiable? Go away, Tate," she mumbled into the down.

A hand shook her shoulder. "Faith. Wake up. Sandy had the baby."

She jerked awake and rolled over. Sunlight beamed through a gap in the curtains, nearly blinding her. Tate sat on the edge of the bed. She'd been dreaming. Good heavens, what had she said? She snatched the sheet to her chin. "What?"

Beard stubble darkened Tate's jaw and his hair stood on end as if he'd just awakened. He looked delicious. Edible. "Our niece has arrived. Want to go and meet her?"

Comprehension dawned. "Anna's here?"

His grin was boyishly sweet and oh, so sexy. "Yeah, all eight pounds of her."

Faith bolted up in the bed and hugged him. The scalding heat of his bare chest permeated her thin gown. She gasped and pulled away, but his hands encircling her waist prevented escape. His green eyes darkened and burned into hers. Air lodged in Faith's lungs and refused to circulate. Her heart pounded and warmth suffused her. Why did he affect her this way when no one else ever had? And why couldn't she just accept today as it came, the way her more liberated friends did, without needing the promise of tomorrows? Because she wanted a family of her own. "Tate—"

"Shh." His mouth covered hers. He sipped from her lips, nuzzled and nipped until she opened for him, and then the kiss turned ravenous. Hot. Slick. Wet. Determined to push him away, she slid her hands over his supple skin, but somehow her fingers ended up threaded through the short, crisp hair of his nape. Her breasts tightened and pushed shamelessly against his chest.

His mouth devoured hers and his hands roamed her back, her waist and finally, he cupped her aching breasts. Faith moaned into his mouth as he plied her flesh. A knot of need formed between her legs. Last night before drifting off to sleep, she'd created a list of reasons why their affair shouldn't be repeated. At this moment, she couldn't recall a thing. She skimmed her nails down his back and reveled in his shiver and groan.

Tate eased her back onto the pillows, following her down. He caught her nipple, gown and all, in his mouth and suckled. One big hand delved beneath the covers, raking up her leg and finding her moist center.

40

He stroked her with unerring accuracy, igniting the embers smoldering inside her until flames of need swept through her. Faith gasped. Her body throbbed. She cradled Tate's bristly face and urged him up for a kiss.

Tate lifted his head and kissed her deeply before drawing back. "You know I'd rather spend the day here with you, but I promised David we'd bring lunch to the hospital within the hour. This afternoon, I'm all yours."

So much for her vow to keep her legs together.

## CHAPTER FIVE

TATE WOULD NEVER understand women. This morning Faith had been hot and *his*. This afternoon, the ice queen had returned. Déjà vu. But her rejection and his resulting confusion didn't stop the persistent throb behind his zipper.

42

In Sandy's hospital room, Tate cradled his tiny niece. The same surge of protectiveness he'd experienced each time his father had placed one of Tate's baby sisters in his arms welled up in him today. His other sisters had married and followed their careers or their husbands' across the country. They lived too far away for Tate to be a hands-on uncle if they ever had children.

As much as he'd once yearned to cast off the responsibility he felt for his sisters, now that they were gone he missed having them underfoot and making demands on his time. He missed being needed. One of these days, he'd like to have kids of his own, but first he had to find a woman who'd have him—a woman who engaged his brain, made him laugh and set his sheets ablaze. Two years ago he hadn't been ready. Now he was.

Was Faith that woman? His gaze met hers and his breath caught at the yearning in her blue eyes. Now *that* he understood. Faith wanted a baby. From what David had told him about Faith's work with children as a physician's assistant, Tate suspected Faith would be a good mother. He crossed the room and stopped before her. "Want to say goodbye to Anna before we get out of here and let David and Sandy get some sleep?"

Faith took the baby from him. Their hands brushed and a jolt of electricity zapped him. She cuddled Anna and cooed nonsense. Something inside Tate shifted, softened. In that instant, he knew he wanted to be the man who fathered Faith's babies. His father's claim that he'd fallen in love with Tate's mother at first sight suddenly seemed plausible. Could love explain this powerful push-pull between Tate and Faith since they'd met? He didn't intend to let the sun set without finding out.

He kissed Sandy's cheek and shook his brother-in-law's hand. "Congratulations. Anna's a beauty. You know I'm only a phone call away if you need anything."

David's grip tightened. He leaned closer and spoke in a low voice. "Remember your toast at our wedding? Ditto. I'll break your legs if you hurt my sister."

Surprised, Tate rocked back on his heels. He looked from David's scowl to Sandy's smile and thumbs-up. Definitely matchmaking. "That's not in my plans." But he did plan to get to the bottom of Faith's deep freeze. He escorted her back to the truck and headed for his apartment. He glanced at the pleat between her brows and the tired shadows beneath her eyes and detoured down the road toward University Lake.

"Where are we going?"

"I thought you might enjoy a rowboat ride. Twice a week, weather permitting, I row laps around the lake. The exercise clears the garbage from my head and gives me a chance to think." The dock was deserted on this overcast day. He parked his truck, rented a boat and rowed them out into the center of the lake. Out here Faith couldn't escape his questions.

Faith broke the silence. "You were very good with Anna." She sat in the bow, facing him.

"Years of practice. Why haven't you married and had kids of your own by now?"

Faith's startled gaze met his. "I've been busy with my training, and I haven't met the right man."

Could he be the right man for Faith? He reconsidered the days leading up to Sandy's wedding. He and Faith had been forced together for most of the events. He'd expected being stuck with her to be a burden. Instead, he'd become addicted to her smiles and her laughter. He'd relished her intelligent, thought-provoking questions. Leaving her each night had grown progressively more difficult, until they'd ended up staying together that last night.

The chemistry between them today was as strong as ever. Each touch and glance packed a wallop. Yeah, he was the right man for Faith King, and if fighting dirty was the only way to get her to admit it, then so be it. "Come here."

Her brows rose. "Excuse me?"

"Sit here. See how relaxing rowing a boat can be." He scooted back on the flat seat, making a space for her between his sprawled legs. His movements rocked the boat.

She gasped and grasped the sides. "I don't think—"

"Don't think. Just come here. It's good exercise. Better than those gym machines you city girls use."

With a distrustful look on her face, she cautiously crawled from her seat to his, turned and scooted into place. "No funny stuff."

"Wouldn't dream of it." He sucked a sharp breath as her butt brushed his groin, and the strawberry scent of her shampoo filled his nostrils. "Grip the oars just above my hands."

She did as he instructed, but her spine remained as rigid as cold steel. "Now what?"

"Follow my moves. Take over when you think you can handle it. Don't drop the oars or they'll fall out of the oarlocks and into the lake, stranding us out here." His bare arms and legs bracketed hers as he rowed them along the water's edge. With each stroke his chest brushed her back and his blood headed south. When Faith took command of the oars, Tate shifted his hands to her waist. She stiffened. "Keep rowing, Faith."

"I said no funny business." Her voice quivered.

He massaged alongside her spine with his thumbs. Her telling shiver was all the encouragement he needed. Lowering his head, he nuzzled aside the collar of her knit shirt and pressed a kiss in the curve of her shoulder. She didn't pull away.

"Tate."

"Shh. Row." He ignored her warning, pushed aside her hair and nibbled her earlobe. Her breath hitched. "Concentrate on keeping your stroke even or we'll turn in circles. Don't lose the oars."

"No fair," she whispered in a breathless middle-of-the-night voice. Her spine curved into his chest, and her fingers tightened on the wooden oar shafts until her knuckles whitened. "Why are you doing this? Why me?"

"Because you melt in my arms each time I touch you and, Faith, you have the same effect on me."

She turned her head, and he saw the uncertainty in her eyes. How could she doubt what she did to him, what they did to each other? He shifted on the narrow seat until her bottom cradled his erection. She gasped and her eyes widened. Her lips eagerly met his. Conscious of their very public location, Tate kept his hands on her waist when he'd much rather drag his palms over her sleek legs and beneath the hem of her shorts or cup her breasts. Their tongues dueled. She bit his bottom lip. His pulse pounded.

*Thud.* He jerked his head back. They'd hit the shore. An overhanging tree provided a thin veil of privacy, but not enough for what he needed. He deepened the kiss and slid his hands higher until his thumbs teased the underside of her breasts. She leaned into his touch. "Let's go back to my place."

She hesitated, and he expected her to chill him out. "Okay."

"You're sure? Faith, if I take you home I'm not going to be happy until I'm inside you."

Faith's eyes closed and her swollen lips parted on a shaky breath. When she lifted her lids, the passion in her blue eyes tempted him to say to hell with waiting until they got home. He wanted her. Here. Now. And damn the consequences.

She licked her lips. "I'm sure."

Tate battled the urge to pull her close and grabbed the oars instead. "Let's go. But do me a favor first. Move back to the bow. If you don't, I have a feeling we might spend the afternoon in jail, and I'd much rather have you in my bed."

BONUS FEATURE

## CHAPTER SIX

SEEING TATE GENTLY CRADLE baby Anna in his big hands had filled Faith with a need so strong she couldn't ignore it. In the park just a short time ago, that need had been matched by a physical desire stronger than any she'd ever known—stronger, even, than it had been during their first meeting.

Who was the real Tate Sumner? The man she'd believed to be Mr. Right had swept her off her feet two years ago, pulled her into the crowd of strangers gathered for David and Sandy's wedding and made her feel right at home. He'd also made Faith feel like the most intelligent and desirable woman on the planet, and he'd made love to her until she couldn't lift her exhausted head off his pillow. She desperately wanted to feel that way again—as if she belonged somewhere and to someone. Did she dare risk it?

But what if the real Tate was the charming womanizer Sandy and her bridesmaids had described? He knew how to push female buttons, the meaning of a Ben & Jerry's Chunky Monkey moment and he liked to play the field. At the wedding he danced with every woman under eighty and made wedding toasts about not settling down until he turned fifty. He, like her father, wouldn't know the meaning of fidelity.

One was the man of her dreams, the other an express train to heartbreak. Would the real Tate Sumner please stand up? Had she completely fooled herself into believing Tate was a family-oriented guy? Could she trust her instincts or was she blinded by the powerful attraction between them? Could she cautiously proceed with Tate, but still guard her heart? How would she know if she didn't take a chance? But she'd witnessed her mother's pain at her father's philandering, and taking that chance scared her spitless.

Tate pulled into his parking space and killed the engine. Faith swallowed the lump in her throat. If she was going to play it safe, then now was the time to call a halt to the proceedings. But what if he was the right man and she let the moment pass?

He turned in his seat and examined her face with a gaze so hot and intense she couldn't breathe. *Wow.* He caressed her jaw with one lightly callused hand and she shivered. Need pooled in her belly. "Changed your mind?"

Her conflicting emotions nearly paralyzed her. She wet her lips and gulped down her doubts. "No."

Tate's fingers tangled in her hair. He pulled her into a kiss so passionate her reservations receded farther out of reach. Faith curled her fingers around his thick biceps and leaned into his chest, reveling in the pressure against her sensitized breasts.

Tate sat back with a groan. "Inside."

He tugged her across the bench seat and out his side of the vehicle. Hand in hand, they hurried into his apartment. As soon as the door closed, Tate pressed her against the wall and kissed her until Faith's knees collapsed. He caught her in his arms and carried her to his bedroom without breaking the kiss, and then set her on her feet beside the bed. Locking his dark green gaze with hers, he reached for the hem of his shirt and yanked the fabric over his head.

Faith mirrored his movements, shucking her shirt, shorts and then shoes. Her heart raced, making her dizzy with desire. This frantic need to get naked was *so* not like her usual cautious self. She paused, wearing only her bra and panties. Was she strong enough to withstand the pain of loving Tate and losing him? Please don't let this be a mistake, she thought to herself.

Tate's gaze burned over her like a flash fire, sweeping her face, her breasts, her legs and back again. "You're more beautiful than I remembered."

Faith's breath hitched. She desperately wanted to believe that wasn't a practiced line. "I'm not beautiful."

"You should see what I see." The gravelly edge to his voice made her tremble.

She visually reacquainted herself with his broad shoulders, narrow waist and washboard abs. Her gaze followed the dark line of hair bisecting his belly to the long, thick ridge barely contained by his briefs. A palm-sized scar on his upper thigh caused her heart to skip a beat. A burn? Had Tate been injured on the job? Her medical training kicked in. The damaged skin was a shiny pink, not red. Not new, but not old enough to have faded to white. Before she could ask her questions, Tate's arms enfolded her, soldering her to the solid heat of his body.

He devoured her mouth with breath-robbing thoroughness while his hands painted a swath of goose bumps over her skin. Faith skated her palms over his muscular back to cup his buttocks. Tate had an amazing butt. He groaned and then planted a line of openmouthed kisses down her neck. He traced the lace of her bra with his tongue and then her bra was gone, and Tate had her in his hot mouth. She tangled her fingers in his hair and fought to stay upright as need twisted inside her.

Surely something that felt this good couldn't be wrong?

His briefs impeded her need to touch him. She shoved the fabric over his hips and then curled her fingers around his hot length. Tate sucked a sharp breath through his teeth, whisked her panties down her legs and found her wetness with devastating, mind-wrecking results. Within moments his deft strokes brought her to the edge of release, held her there for several heart-pounding moments and then pushed her over. Faith collapsed against him, gasping and clinging to his shoulders.

Tate pressed a hard, swift kiss on her lips and then put a few inches between them. He reached into the bedside drawer for protection, which he quickly donned, and then he fell back on the bed, pulling her over him like a blanket. Her thighs straddled his hips and his erection teased her core. She slid against him, teasing him and herself. His splayed fingers cradled her bottom, stilling her motions.

"You're killing me, Faith. I need to be inside you," he said through clenched teeth.

She'd never had a lover who made her feel as powerful, womanly or needed. Faith curled her fingers around him and lowered one excruciating inch at a time. His growl drowned out her gasp as he filled her. Tate's grip on her hips tightened, and he surged upward, driving deeper and faster. His hands found her breasts, tweaking her until she felt as taut as an over-wound clock. She braced herself against his chest, clutched his shoulders and held on as pleasure built inside her. Tate tangled his fingers in her hair and tugged her down for an explosive kiss that mimicked his thrusting. His hand shifted to the joining of their bodies. Faith climbed higher and higher with every stroke until she tumbled off the summit in a free fall of rapture. Tate arched off the bed and groaned against her neck as shudders racked him.

Her muscles turned fluid, too weak to remain upright. Tate eased her down beside him, tucking her head into his shoulder and kissing her brow. The room fell silent except for their labored breathing. When they were together like this, she could almost forget her doubts and fears. Could she trust a charmer like Tate to remain faithful? The overhead ceiling fan cooled Faith's sweat-dampened skin, and her pulse returned to normal. Tate's breath slowed and evened out.

Had she found her soul mate or was she just in heat? She could almost hear her best friend ask, "Is being in heat a bad thing?" Not if she remembered it was temporary. But Faith didn't want temporary. She wanted a family. She wanted forever. And she wanted both with Tate. The knowledge scared her and left her vulnerable. She didn't want to go through life alone, but loving Tate meant opening herself up to pain, loss and betrayal.

Faith dragged her hand down Tate's chest to the scar on his leg. It was superficial and not at all unsightly, but it was a warning flag—a reminder that even if Tate wasn't a womanizer, she could lose him all the same. The scar was proof that he could be taken from her at any time, and love, that fleeting emotion, offered no guarantees of happiness.

BONUS FEATURE

Did she really want to lose her heart and risk the pain? The weight on her chest told her she already had.

Was it too late to repair the damage?

54

## CHAPTER SEVEN

TATE ROLLED OVER in bed. Empty. He squinted at his alarm clock. He'd slept like the dead for hours. He tossed off the sheet and sat up. "Faith?"

No answer. Where was she? He crawled from the bed, checked the bathroom, the kitchen and the deck overlooking the pool. No Faith. The same clammy clench he'd felt before entering the building that had fallen in on him, squeezed his gut. Intuition? Tate retraced his steps and looked in his closet and drawer. Her stuff was gone.

"Dammit. This hot/cold thing is getting old."

He yanked back the curtains. She must have called a taxi because his truck was in its usual spot. How in the hell had he slept through her leaving? Blame it on too many twenty-four-hour shifts covering end-of-the-year fraternity parties. Tate dug his cell phone out of the pants he'd shed beside his bed and punched speed dial for David's number. As soon as his brother-in-law answered, Tate asked, "Is Faith with you?"

"No, she left here with you. What have you done to my sister, Tate?"

He understood David's anger. "Nothing." Except fall in love with her. He massaged the knots forming in the back of his neck. "Call my cellular if you hear from her. Please."

"Find her."

"I will. Count on it." He disconnected and made another pass through his apartment, this time searching for clues. Where could she have gone? He found the phone book on the kitchen counter open to the *S* section of the hotel listings and swore. Thanks to all the graduation ceremonies going on this week, the sleazy Streetside was the only hotel in town with rooms available. Was Faith willing to put herself in danger to get away from him?

Tate lifted the phone and called a police officer buddy he'd known since high school. He'd take months of ribbing for his request, but he didn't know what else to do. "Jay, I need a favor. My sister-in-law has taken off. I need to find her. Her name is Faith King. Thirty-one. Strawberry-blonde. Blue eyes. Medium height. Start with the Streetside Hotel."

"Did she do anything illegal?"

Could their encounters be classified as *hit and run?* His heart sure felt as if it had been run over. "Nothing you'd be interested in."

"Want me to bring her in?"

"No. Just locate her and don't let her leave before I get there. For God's sake keep her safe if she's in that dump."

Thirty minutes later, Tate parked his truck beside Jay's cruiser in the hotel parking lot. Jay led him toward the back of the hotel. "She checked in ninety minutes ago. Room six."

"I owe you, man."

"Pizza and a beer should cover your debt, but I'm gonna want details later. You're usually a little smoother with the ladies." Jay motioned Tate away from the hotel's paint-chipped door. "Step aside, Sumner. If you've pissed her off she's not going to open the door for you, but she'll open it for me."

Tate sighed and flattened himself against the wall a few feet away. The fact that he'd made a fool of himself over a woman would be all over Chapel Hill in a matter of hours, but it'd be worth it if he could work this out with Faith. Whatever *this* was. Was it love? What else could explain the sinking feeling in his gut?

"Deal."

"And don't do anything stupid or, friend or not, I'll have to run you in." Jay offered the last warning as he lifted his fist and rapped on the door.

The door eased open. Tate heard the chain catch. At least, she'd had sense enough to use it.

"Faith King?" Jay asked.

"Yes." Tate hated the fear in her voice. He'd forgotten Jay's ugly mug could make the *Godfather* thugs look like beauty contestants.

"Step outside, Ms. King."

"Is there a problem, Officer?"

"That's what I want to know."

The door closed. The chain scraped, and then the door reopened. Faith stepped out onto the cracked sidewalk. Tate's heart slammed against his ribs. She turned her head, spotted him and her eyes widened. "What's wrong? Are David, Sandy and Anna okay?"

"Your family is fine, but Sumner needs to talk to you." Jay indicated Tate.

A different kind of tension entered her face. "I don't think we have anything to say."

Tate smothered his anger, his pain. "You can't keep running, Faith."

Her chin lifted, revealing that telling red spot at the base of her throat. "I'm not running."

Jay's radio squawked. "Can you two handle this now? I have a call."

"Yes. Thanks again, Jay," Tate replied.

"There's nothing to handle," Faith said simultaneously, but Jay had already turned toward his cruiser. Seconds later he hit the siren and peeled out of the lot.

"What are you afraid of?" Tate stepped closer.

The quarter-sized spot on her skin glowed like a streetlight. "Nothing."

Tate circled the splotch on her chest with his finger. "This says otherwise."

She flinched out of reach. Covering her chest with her hand, she backed into her room. "Go away, Tate."

Tate followed, kicking the door shut and sealing them in the seedy hotel room. "I rescue people from danger. I don't leave them in harm's way. I'm not leaving you here."

"Why can't you accept that we had a one-night stand and let it go? You should thank me for not asking for more."

His heart thumped harder and his mouth dried. "Ask."

Her lips parted and her eyes widened. Wh-what?"

"Ask for more, Faith."

"I don't want more." The desire in her eyes and the hunger in her lips when she loved him said otherwise.

"You're not a no-strings kind of woman."

"Says you, and you barely know me. Tate, we've only known each other a week total."

"I can accept it if you think we're moving too fast and you need more time, but I won't accept your refusal to give us a chance."

He saw the flash of fear in her eyes before she looked away. "I can't. Go back to your other women…and your job."

*Fear?* This was all about fear? He remembered her touching the scar on his leg as he drifted off to sleep. He'd thought Faith up to the challenge of being a firefighter's wife. Evidently, he'd been wrong.

"I never expected you to be a coward, Faith."

## CHAPTER EIGHT

"YOU THINK I'm a coward?" Faith's skin prickled at the accuracy of Tate's remark.

Tate shrugged. "If the shoe fits…"

"I have good reason to be cautious."

He widened his stance and parked his hands on his hips. "And that is…?"

Where did she start? "Did David ever tell you about our father?"

"Only that he was a jerk."

Faith winced. "He's a pilot with charm and good looks to spare. He has a woman in every layover city. My mother knew about his infidelities and it broke her heart. I don't want to live like that. I don't want to love a man who'll hurt me over and over and not care."

His brows dipped and his shoulders squared. "You're comparing me to your father?"

"That night before the wedding, I was well on my way to falling in love with you, but you were playing a game. The next day at the church you flirted with every female present."

He made an exasperated sound. "Only because you blew me off."

"Are you denying you'd had a reputation for keeping your affairs short and sweet?"

Tate shoved a hand through his hair, making his cowlick stand up. "No."

"And were you expecting more than a brief affair after Sandy and David's wedding?"

His jaw muscles bunched. "No."

Faith exhaled slowly and hugged herself. Well, nothing like hearing your fears confirmed. "That's what your sister and her bridesmaids told me. They took bets on which wedding guest would be foolish enough to fall for your charms. I was too ashamed to tell them that I already had."

62

"Remind me to muzzle my sisters." Tate crossed the room, stopping inches away. His woodsy cologne teased Faith's senses, and his serious green gaze held hers. "As far back as I can remember, I was the man of the house. I filled in when my dad was on duty, and after his death my mother and my sisters looked to me to keep things normal. I gave up my dreams of college, and signed on as a firefighter because we needed the money to put my sisters through college. I resented the hell out of it. I was young and all I wanted was to party and get laid. Hell, I was twenty before I lost my virginity.

"Sandy was the last of my sisters to leave home. When Sandy met your brother the year before they married I thought I'd finally found freedom, and I was determined to make up for lost time. I tried." He shook his head with a rueful smile on his face. "God, I tried. Then I met you, and I panicked. You made me want more than just hot sex. You threatened my newfound freedom. When you blew me off after our night together, I was angry and decided to show you that I didn't care. I wanted to make you jealous, and I wanted to make sure you knew what you were missing. I'm sorry. I was an ass at the reception."

"Yes, you were." But hearing the reasons why gave her a new perspective.

He grimaced. "You were the right woman for me, Faith, but I was too stupid to recognize it. Give me a chance now to show you how right we are together, and I promise you won't regret it."

Her heart missed a beat, but fear held her back. "How can I trust you not to hurt me? I need someone who'll love me forever, Tate, not just when it's convenient."

"There are no guarantees in life. You have to set aside your fears or they'll paralyze you."

That's exactly what had happened. Faith yearned for a family of her own, and yet she never dated a man more than a few times. As soon as she began to grow attached, she broke off the relationship. She'd been envious as her friends married and found happiness, but Faith was afraid to try it for herself. The one time she had—with Tate—she'd been burned.

"Even if you're not as fickle as my father, any fire call you answer could be your last. Your leg…" She motioned to his thigh and bit her lip as fear choked off her words.

"Any time you get in your car to drive to work could be your last trip, but you won't see me locking you in my apartment. I won't deny my job can be hazardous. I was injured in a building collapse because I ignored my training and entered an unstable situation. I figured I had nothing to lose. Now I do." He brushed a soft kiss over her lips.

Faith's breath caught and her resistance ebbed. "You make me weak, Tate. I tell myself not to fall for your charm or your lines, and then I do anyway. Do you know my only goal for this weekend was to keep my knees together around you? And I failed."

His tender smile tugged at her heartstrings. He lifted a hand and cupped her jaw. "That's because your heart knows better than your head. And you're not weak, Faith. The woman I see when we're together is one who knows what she wants and takes it. It's your follow-through that needs work."

"I'm afraid of being wrong, of being hurt." And she was afraid of being alone, but wasn't she alone now?

"I run into burning buildings for a living, but nothing scares me as much as losing you." Tate pulled her into his arms and kissed her deeply. Faith clung to his broad shoulders. Hope flickered to life inside her.

64

The unmistakable banging of a headboard on the adjoining wall startled them apart. Moans of passion followed. Tate released her and grabbed her suitcase.

"Let's get out of here. I'll be damned if I'll propose in this dump."

Faith's heart stopped and her mouth fell open. "You're going to propose?"

Tate yanked open the door and paused on the threshold. "I guess the only way you'll know for sure is if you find the guts to come with me."

The door swung shut behind him. Faith stood in the center of the sleazy room paralyzed by indecision. She wanted a husband who always put family first, a man who made her feel womanly and wise. She needed a man brave enough to fight his own demons and hers.

She pressed a hand over her thumping heart. Tate Sumner was that man. He offered the love she'd dreamed of and wanted more than anything else in the world, but she had to find the courage to seize it before it was too late. He hadn't said he loved her. Did he? Suddenly, Faith had to find out. She picked up her purse and followed him out. She had so much to lose, but so much more to gain. She was ready to put her heart on the line.

Tate helped her into his pickup truck without a word. Neither of them spoke as he drove toward the lake and parked in the shade. He climbed from the cab and headed toward a big boulder on the lake's edge. Faith followed and stood beside him on trembling legs as he stood gazing out over the wind-whipped water.

"My father claimed he fell in love with my mother at first sight. As a kid I thought that was the dumbest thing I'd ever heard," Tate said without looking at her, and then he turned his head and Faith's breath stalled in her lungs at the love in his eyes. He took her hands in his. "And then I met you, and I knew exactly what he meant. I love you, Faith, and I promise you that I'll keep on loving you until the day I die."

Emotion welled within her, spilling from her eyes in big, fat tears. "I love you, too."

"Marry me. Today. Tomorrow. Whenever you can trust in what I feel for you."

A watery smile wobbled on her lips. "I trust in your love now, and I think today or tomorrow or as soon as we can arrange it would be perfect."

Note: Originally published online at www.eHarlequin.com

**HOTEL MARCHAND**

**Four sisters.
A family legacy.
And someone is out to destroy it.**

---

**A captivating new limited
continuity, launching June 2006**

---

The most beautiful hotel in New Orleans,
and someone is out to destroy it. But mystery,
danger and some surprising family revelations
and discoveries won't stop the Marchand sisters
from protecting their birthright…
and finding love along the way.

# Paying the Playboy's Price

(Silhouette Desire #1732)

## by

# EMILIE ROSE

Juliana Alden is determined to have her last—
her only—fling before settling down. And she's
found the perfect candidate: bachelor Rex Tanner.
He's pure playboy charm…but can she afford
his price?

**Trust Fund Affairs:** They've just spent a fortune—
the bachelors had better be worth it.

### Don't miss the other titles in this series:

EXPOSING THE EXECUTIVE'S SECRETS (July)
BENDING TO THE BACHELOR'S WILL (August)

### On sale this June from Silhouette Desire.

*Available wherever books are sold, including most
bookstores, supermarkets, discount stores and drugstores.*

If you enjoyed what you just read,
then we've got an offer you can't resist!

# Take 2 bestselling love stories FREE!

# Plus get a FREE surprise gift!

**Clip this page and mail it to Harlequin Reader Service®**

| IN U.S.A. | IN CANADA |
|---|---|
| 3010 Walden Ave. | P.O. Box 609 |
| P.O. Box 1867 | Fort Erie, Ontario |
| Buffalo, N.Y. 14240-1867 | L2A 5X3 |

**YES!** Please send me 2 free Harlequin Romance® novels and my free surprise gift. After receiving them, if I don't wish to receive anymore, I can return the shipping statement marked cancel. If I don't cancel, I will receive 6 brand-new novels every month, before they're available in stores! In the U.S.A., bill me at the bargain price of $3.57 plus 25¢ shipping & handling per book and applicable sales tax, if any*. In Canada, bill me at the bargain price of $4.05 plus 25¢ shipping & handling per book and applicable taxes**. That's the complete price and a savings of 10% off the cover prices—what a great deal! I understand that accepting the 2 free books and gift places me under no obligation ever to buy any books. I can always return a shipment and cancel at any time. Even if I never buy another book from Harlequin, the 2 free books and gift are mine to keep forever.

186 HDN DZ72
386 HDN DZ73

| Name | (PLEASE PRINT) | |
|---|---|---|
| Address | Apt.# | |
| City | State/Prov. | Zip/Postal Code |

**Not valid to current Harlequin Romance® subscribers.**
**Want to try another series? Call 1-800-873-8635**
**or visit www.morefreebooks.com.**

\* Terms and prices subject to change without notice. Sales tax applicable in N.Y.
\*\* Canadian residents will be charged applicable provincial taxes and GST.
  All orders subject to approval. Offer limited to one per household.
  ® are registered trademarks owned and used by the trademark owner or its licensee.

HROM04R                                    ©2004 Harlequin Enterprises Limited

## HARLEQUIN®

# *American* ROMANCE®

## IS PROUD TO PRESENT A GUEST APPEARANCE BY

QUILL
BOOK
AWARD
WINNING
AUTHOR

*NEW YORK TIMES* bestselling author

# DEBBIE MACOMBER

## *The Wyoming Kid*

The story of an ex–rodeo cowboy,
a schoolteacher and their journey to the altar.

"Best-selling Macomber, with more than
100 romances and women's fiction titles
to her credit, sure has a way of pleasing readers."
—*Booklist* on *Between Friends*

**The Wyoming Kid is available from
Harlequin American Romance in July 2006.**